MW00911639

The Hagenspan Chronicles

Book Four

Roarke's Wisdom

The Last Dragon

Robert W. Tompkins

Roarke's Wisdom

The Last Dragon

translated from the original tongues by

Robert W. Tompkins

Roarke's Wisdom

Book Four: The Last Dragon

being chiefly concerned with the events which occurred in County Temter

Hatred.

Ha!

Glorious, gorious, horious hatred.
Blest, best, beating in our breast.

> *Stomp and crush! Bite and eat!*

Love.

Ha! Ha!

Simpering, whimpering, pimpering love.

> *Stomp and crush! Rend and tear! Bite and eat!*

Tender mercies of fools.
They shall be utterly mashed.

> *Stomp and crush! Rend and tear!*

Everything I see is mine.
I am all that there is.

> *Stomp and crush!*

Chapter One

"Did you see anything on the other side of the trees?"

Alan Poppleton was sweating profusely in his suit of armor, but he was loath to take it off, since he felt that he *must* be getting close to the dragon by now.

Alan's squire, Brette, looked with concern at his master. "Alan, you really should take off that armor, dry yourself off, and get into something warm. You're going to catch the ague or something."

Brette was actually only a year younger than Alan, and the two had been friends for their entire lives. But Alan was the son of old Lord Poppleton, and Brette was just the son of one of Poppleton's retainers. When Alan had made the decision to ride to the defense of Solemon, though, Brette refused to be left behind, and Alan had welcomed his company. The pair had left Ester without telling their fathers, for fear that they would be denied; they had left notes saying that they had gone to visit Castle Thraill, which technically was true.

"Did you see anything?" Alan repeated.

"Just an open plain. Lots of grass. I'm not sure," Brette said doubtfully. "I think we're lost."

"Well, we couldn't be *very* lost," Alan groused. "We just keep heading east, and sooner or later we have to either find the King's Road or else the Maur Wain. Even if we can't find Solemon itself, we can make our way there as long as we keep heading east."

"Yeah," Brette admitted, "I guess." He thought for a few minutes. "Are you sure that river we crossed this morning isn't the Maur Wain?"

"Maybe. But I think it's the Eldric." He mopped his brow with a corner of his horse's saddle blanket. "I don't know."

"Well, if we keep on heading east, and we come to the Great Sea, we probably ought to turn around and head west for a bit."

Alan offered a febrile grin and said, "If we come to the Sea, that's what we'll do." He leaned against a tree. "Maybe you're right about taking a rest. Can you help me unbuckle this thing?"

While Brette was helping unfasten the brassards from the breastplate, he said, "Just sit and rest, Alan. I'll put together a little fire and make us a bite."

"Thank you ... I'm feeling a bit poorly."

Sir Fentin and Sir Jayles led a procession of twenty men northward on the King's Road from Ruric's Keep to Solemon. Off to the west, a thin column of smoke arose from the forest that surrounded the headwaters of the Eldric River. Probably some refugees from Solemon, hiding out, trying to secure a place of shelter for the winter. They were everywhere, little knots of huddled people who had fled from their homes and now had nowhere to call their own. The forest was as good a place as any to try and hole up until the dragon was vanquished.

The men that accompanied Jayles and Fentin were understandably nervous, but felt that they had some reason for confidence. It had been several weeks since King Ruric's call to arms had gone out, and they believed that several waves of volunteers had preceded them to Solemon. And while those warriors had apparently not yet been successful in utterly defeating their foe—no word to that effect had been delivered to the king—they must at *least* be wearing the beast down, injuring it, weakening it. Besides which, Jayles and Fentin were transporting a new weapon, a new invention of the king's own conception, which they believed would finally deliver the killing blow to the serpent.

King Ruric, in hopes of protecting the lives of as many of his men as he could, had advocated the use of arrows instead of swords in order to keep as much distance as possible between the men and their adversary. When told that arrows seemed to just glance off the beast harmlessly, he had thought to himself that perhaps what was needed were bigger arrows. He had then commissioned engineers to quickly design a huge bow that rode on a horse-drawn framework, lying upon its side, from which arrows the size of small trees could be propelled with devastating force. The test firing of the first trial construction had completely destroyed one stone wall in an inner courtyard at Ruric's Keep, to the exuberant cheering of the knights remaining at the castle.

Two of the giant crossbows had been built, and were on their way now to Solemon behind Fentin and Jayles, who had been granted the honor of securing the victory for the king. Since the huge projectiles used in the mechanisms were heavy and slow to load, only six of the tree-like arrows had been produced. Two of the six arrows had metal tips, which cost much time and expense to fashion; the other four had been sharpened like stakes on their tips. It took a team of six men to load the crossbow and launch the shaft, and, once readied to fire, the bow could not be easily repositioned. So, besides Fentin and Jayles, and the dozen men required to operate the two weapons, there were also two teams of three men each whose perilous duty it was to engage the dragon in conventional battle and lure it to a spot where it would be within the range of the crossbows.

The men who rode with Jayles and Fentin spoke in low tones among themselves. They imagined being greeted with hurrahs by the beleaguered men who defended Solemon, who were perhaps hiding in abandoned buildings or behind hastily-constructed ramparts. They hoped the dragon was still on its feet, so that they would be the ones who received the honor of killing it at last, receiving a share in whatever reward would be given by the king to the victors. The men who were to be stationed behind the crossbows seemed to be somewhat more optimistic than those who were charged with goading the dragon.

Jubal wished he had never heard of the dragon, wished he had never heard King Ruric's call for volunteers, wished he had never left Blythecairne. He wished bitterly that he had never left home and gone to seek his fortune at Blythecairne in the first place.

Lying under the pile of debris where he had hidden himself, he felt ashamed of his conduct. Somehow, miraculously, the dragon had not found him. He had heard the huge reptile thundering down the street behind him, had heard the scream of a horse, heard thrashing and guttural snarling and cracking of bones. But he had stayed still and hidden, and apparently the dragon had not been able to follow his scent.

So … what to do now?

He was weaponless and impotent. He was terrified and hungry and alone and beginning to shiver from the cold.

He could try to sneak out of Solemon and walk back to Blythecairne, maybe, and tell them that the danger was even greater than they had believed. Or he could go back to the center of town and try to connect with those boys who had been on the tops of the buildings. Maybe they had weapons. Maybe they had food. Maybe they had some kind of idea what to do.

As quietly as he could, Jubal disentangled himself from the fragments of wrecked housing materials that he had secreted himself beneath. Apparently the sun had nearly set, because a gray pall covered his hiding place and long shadows draped themselves across the street like a spider's web. He cast a cautious glance up the street toward the town square, and saw nothing moving, so he began creeping warily in that direction.

He was just beginning to dare to hope that the boys on the rooftops might have something hot to eat when he heard a soft snort, and felt a puff of breath on the back of his neck.

Chapter Two

The morning broke crisp and bright, and Roarke woke feeling refreshed, cheerful, even happy. He prayed, "Thank You for the gift of this day," even as he realized that there might not be very many more, not for him. He thought about his own attitude for a moment, wondering if he shouldn't rather be feeling depressed or regretful, wondered if maybe he were becoming slightly unbalanced, and decided that it didn't matter. He wanted to sing.

As he put together a small cold breakfast, he hummed his morning song, noticing ruefully that it wasn't quite so easy for him to hold the tune steady as it was when he was younger, but he figured that God probably didn't care much about that.

He sat and ate with his back resting against a small tree. He watched Justice grazing contentedly on grass dewy with freshly melting frost. He studied the grass itself and was surprised at how clearly he could see each blade, if he just paused long enough to look at it. Cobwebs shone in the morning sunlight like tiny glistening tapestries, and birds sang their own cheerful morning choruses, darting bits of color in the undergrowth.

Roarke was quietly amazed at the beautiful sights, the beautiful sounds ... the beautiful world. His belly was satisfied, his eyes were full, his ears too. The air was cold against his cheeks, but he liked it. As hard as he might try (and he didn't try very hard), he could not make himself feel fear or regret about his impending encounter with the dragon.

He prayed silently. *What a good morning, Almighty.* He could see some small yellowish-brown animal creeping around in the brush, and wondered if it might be a stoat. *I know I haven't been as regular in my prayers as I used to be, not since you gave me Hollie. But I didn't mean to be ungrateful ... it's just that I was enjoying myself so much.* The little brown creature stuck its head out of the brush and sat up, looking at the horse, who was an unwelcome stranger in its environment. Maybe it was some other kind of weasel.

"Good morning, friend," Roarke said softly. The weasel's head snapped to face Roarke, who continued to speak in soothing tones. "What a morning God has given us, yes?" Maybe it was a ferret. "This must be your world, yes? And we are the intruders. Well, we'll be gone in a little bit, and then you can go back to your hunting." The weasel continued to watch Roarke, unmoving but for twitching whiskers. "We're going hunting, too. My last time. If I can come back from this one, I intend to sit in a chair until I grow great and fat, and I shall only rise in order to kiss my wife or my son." The weasel, apparently deciding that Roarke was not a threat, started to rustle around in the grass as if looking for something. "Well, I thank you for your company this morning, little friend."

Roarke returned to his prayers. *I do thank You for the beauties of this day, God. Is this what it's like every day in Your country? Cool and bracing, full of things to delight the eyes and the imagination? I can't even begin....* Roarke thought about the book of God's words, the *Iesuchristion*, and wondered if he would live long enough to hear what those words meant. *But*, he thought, *perhaps I will see for myself, instead of being told.*

He stood stiffly to his feet, feeling like rusted metal. He smiled faintly. *God ... if it would please You to let me defeat this one last dragon, then ... well, it would please me, too. If You have other plans ... well, I suppose You are wiser than I am. If this coming fight is to be my doorway to Your country, then I just ask, most humbly, that You would welcome me as Your friend. Foolish old man that I am.*

He picked up his saddle and equipment from the grass where it lay next to Justice, and began outfitting the horse. *Maybe Your land is better*

8

than mine, he thought. *Maybe it's preferable to be in Your world than it is to be here. But this is the only world that I know, and everything that I love is here.* He thought of Hollie, of Owan, of Willum. *But ... I will trust You.*

Not knowing what else to do, he mounted his horse and began heading eastward.

Chapter Three

Riding a horse was the most thrilling thing that King of the Dragon had ever done, with the possible exception of the undeniably courageous act of facing the silent dragon in the Cave of Mendor. He clung tightly to the horse's mane with his little gray fists as Sir Willum led them across the sparse plain toward the forlorn region which was called the Northern Wastelands, when it was called anything at all.

The two explorers had traveled for several days without seeing any signs of life bigger than birds or small rodents. King of the Dragon didn't recognize any of the terrain as belonging to his own past, but then it had been twenty years since he had been beyond the sight of Mendor. A few times he had ventured a tentative, "That looks familiar," only to concede a moment later, "Well, I guess not."

But even though the pair was not having success with their objective of trying to find a family for the King, their spirits were high. Will was enjoying the adventure of surveying the northern wastes, which even Roarke had never seen.

And the King was enjoying Will's company, Will's food, and riding the horse.

r

Tilda and Vesta, their nostrils twitching as they sniffed the breeze, watched warily as the four horses approached. Two of the horses were laden only with packs, but the one in the lead bore a huge rider, and on the mount behind him was one of their own, apparently a prisoner of the big fellow. They exchanged ominous glances, their eyes flaring red. They had been foraging for food in preparation for the coming winter, but they had not expected to find this alarming situation ... whatever it was.

Tilda, who was the elder, whispered to his companion, "How's aboot chunkin' a rock at yonder rider, an' mebbe we can free our poor nekkid brother there."

Vesta nodded hopefully and hefted a large stone. "Ye think he's good t' eat?" he said, meaning Will.

"We'll find oot, mebbe. Them 'osses will be."

Vesta stepped from behind the boulder where they were hiding, and with a determined grunt sent the stone hurtling in the direction of Willum. He had underestimated the weight of the stone, though, as well as overestimating his own strength, and the stone thudded harmlessly on the ground several yards from Will. The young knight steered Starlight in the direction of the attack to see Vesta standing there, wearing an astonished look on his gray face.

Will thought to himself that the little creature who had thrown the stone had to be the same kind of being as King of the Dragon, though he was certainly better clothed than the King. He raised a tentative hand in salute and called, "Don't fear! I mean ye no harm!"

Vesta stared mutely for part of a moment, his jaw hanging slack, then found his voice and cried, "Bats!"

"I don't get yer meanin'," Will said cautiously.

"Bats! If ye threaten me, I'll call all th' bats o' Hell down on yer head! I can, ye know!"

From his hiding place behind the boulder, Tilda chuckled and said, "Bats. That's a good 'un."

"I won't threaten ye. How many of ye are there?" Will asked, hearing Tilda but not seeing him.

"Oh, hunnerts," Vesta said vaguely. "Ye're surrounded, mostly."

King of the Dragon spoke up. "Don't loose no bats on him. This is Sir Willum, an' he's a friend, an' under my pertection."

"A friend? Ye mean ye ain't his prisoner?"

"O' course not. What'd ye think that fer?"

"Well, ye're nekkid, fer one, an' ye ain't leadin' yer own 'oss, fer another. If he's yer friend, why'd he let ye ride around on a led 'oss with yer doodle hangin' oot?"

"This is what I allus wear," King of the Dragon said reluctantly, and suddenly the thought occurred to him that he might not like being reunited with his own people as much as he had hoped.

"Well ... arright," Vesta agreed. "But ain't ye cold?"

"Yes, a mite."

"What d'ye want here in these parts?" Tilda cried from his hiding place.

"We were looking for you," Will said. "My friend has been alone for a long time, and we were hoping to find his family, if they still live here."

"Yer family, eh?" Tilda stepped out from behind the boulder. "What's yer name?"

King of the Dragon swallowed nervously, his eyes darting from one to the other, and said, "I don't rightly recall. Sir Willum calls me 'King o' th' Dragon.'"

"That ain't a name!" Vesta snorted derisively. "We'll call ye … 'Doodle.'"

"That ain't a name, neither." King of the Dragon's eyes flared crimson.

"Is, so," said Vesta. "Yers."

Tilda interjected, "Mebbe 'Doodle' ain't much of a name, but 'King o' th' Dragon' ain't neither. An' facts is facts: ye ain't king o' nothin' here in these parts. So ye might's well be 'Doodle.'"

King of the Dragon said to Will in a low voice, "I don't know's I like these fellers so well."

Will said, "Let's talk to 'em for a bit. Maybe they'll lighten up on ye."

"I don't know," the King grumbled.

Will said to Tilda and Vesta, "Might we share a meal with ye, and get yer counsel on where we should go from here?"

"Aye, that'd be arright," Tilda said, brightening.

"I don't know if we've got enough to feed all of yer companions, but if they'd like to join us—"

"Nah, that's arright," Vesta replied. "They can eat somethin' else." Willum dismounted and helped King of the Dragon down from his horse.

ʃ

The four sat around a campfire that had been built by Vesta. King of the Dragon had watched in awe as Vesta constructed the fire, saying, "Ye mean ye know how t' make a *far*?"

"Who don't?" Vesta replied carelessly.

"Not me," King of the Dragon said offhandedly. "I was jest surprised that *you* fellers knew how to."

After the meal, which was punctuated frequently by satisfied grunts and belches, Will asked a question that he had been curious about ever since he had first met King of the Dragon. Hoping not to offend the small gray creatures, he said, "Just what kind of folk *are* ye boys, anyway?"

"Ye mean ye don't even know what kind o' bein' ye *are*?" Vesta asked King of the Dragon, amazed.

"I was allus jest *me*," the King said glumly. "Never occurred t' me that there was other kind o' folk besides what I was, an' then when it did, there weren't no one t' ask."

Tilda answered Will's question. "Well, our blood ain't pure no more— whose is?—but mostly, we're descended from kobolds. Some of our gran'parents was pure kobold, but that was a long time ago, some generations back." He looked at King of the Dragon kindly. "What do ye know aboot kobolds, Doodle?"

"Nothin' yet."

Relating the history of his people was a source of some pleasure to Tilda, so he fluffed his clothing, making himself more comfortable, and began speaking in a pedantic tone. "The kobolds is a wonderful batch o' folk, tender-hearted an' helpful t' their friends, an' dangerous as a snake t' their foes. Our gran'parents, years an' years ago, was smaller folk than us, 'cause our blood got mixed with human blood, an' it made us bigger an' not so clever as we once was."

Will thought that it was highly unlikely that a normal human would ever want to mate with one of these creatures. Before he could stop himself, he blurted, "How?"

"Our gran'parents was ever so shy, not usually showin' themselves around too much. Quiet, reserved folk. Mostly they'd sneak inta people's huts when they was asleep, an' do little chores t' help 'em oot, an' mebbe play little tricks on 'em an' such. Well, some of th' kobolds took advantage o' bein' under th' cover o' darkness, no doubt, an' sneck in on th' people whilst they was dreamin'. Ain't much more that needs t' be said aboot that. Anyways, our bloods got mixed."

"Oh."

"As th' years went by, humans quit appreciatin' all th' help we give 'em, an' jest started complainin' aboot th' pranks. 'Where's my axe?' they'd say. 'How'd th' milk get spoilt?' An' so the kobolds took t' spendin' less an' less time helpin' 'em oot, an' started livin' in caves an' amongst th' barren places o' th' world, 'stead o' livin' amongst th' humans.

"Nowadays, it's a rare thing t' be around humans at all. Most kobolds cain't stand bein' around 'em. I expect it's 'cause o' th' smell," he said apologetically, "though ye seem t' be a kindly sort, fer a human."

"Thank ye," Will said humbly.

Tilda continued, "Well, what's *yer* story, Doodle? How'd ye come t' be alone?"

King of the Dragon said grimly, "I expect I don't know. All I recall is that there was wolves, an' my ma said t' run, an' so I did."

"Oh, yes, the wolves," Tilda said. "That was a bad time."

Vesta asked King of the Dragon, "So, Doodle ... are ye plannin' on stayin' here an' livin' with us?"

King of the Dragon turned to Willum with a desperate look in his yellow eyes.

Vesta continued, "'Cause we could use another hand helpin' us find food fer th' winter. Our people is mighty hungry, an' some of 'em'll be dyin' afore spring comes again."

Tilda addressed Will. "One o' them 'osses would be right helpful."

Vesta said, "Aye. If ye get t' keep one o' yer 'osses," he said to King of the Dragon, "mebbe we'll even let ye be th' king o' somethin'."

Will said, "The King and I need to talk about these things before we make a decision." King of the Dragon smiled at him gratefully. "Would you two gents like to share a camp with us tonight?"

ʔ

When Will and King of the Dragon woke in the morning, the two packhorses were gone, and Tilda and Vesta were nowhere to be found.

King of the Dragon said sadly, "I guess them boys didn't want me stayin' here after all."

"Maybe not."

The little kobold was silent for a few moments. "Would ye still be askin' me t' go t' yer Castle Thraill?" he said forlornly.

"Of course, Yer Majesty, if ye wish."

"Sir Willum?"

"Yes, Yer Majesty?"

"Would ye help me know how t' wear clothes?"

"It would be my honor to show you what I know."

King of the Dragon smiled feebly. After thinking a moment more, he spoke again. "Sir Willum?"

"Yes," Will nodded.

"Ye won't call me 'Doodle,' will ye?"

"No, Yer Highness. Ye'll always be the King to me."

He smiled again, a little more sincerely. "Thankee."

The two had breakfast, then shared the chores of striking the camp. Will helped the King back onto his horse, and they started back on their southward journey into Hagenspan.

After traveling in silence for about an hour, King of the Dragon chuckled faintly, and said, "'Doodle.' That's purty funny, ain't it?"

Will looked at his friend. "No, Yer Majesty."

King of the Dragon smiled gratefully, and said, "Thankee, Sir Willum."

Chapter Four

Fentin, Jayles, and the men who followed them clattered up the road toward the southern edge of Solemon. Fentin and Jayles exchanged concerned looks. Where were the other warriors? There was evidence of battle, some of it grisly and frightening, but there were no living men or beasts anywhere that they could see.

Including the dragon. Where was that?

Fentin said quietly, "Perhaps the battle has shifted deeper into the town." No sounds of combat could be heard, though—just the ethereal moaning of the wind, a barren, bleak whine.

"Yes," Jayles said doubtfully. If it was necessary for them to maneuver the large crossbows down streets, around buildings ... Jayles silently questioned whether they would be able to use them at all. Perhaps they should load the weapons now and aim them toward the center of the street, between the houses at the end of town, and then send the men into Solemon to see if they could lure the dragon back down here. He voiced the thought to Fentin.

"Yes ... that would solve the problem of trying to get the bows into the town. They'd have to go single file on the street, and then what good would the second one be anyway?" The silence emanating from Solemon like an audible thing was unnerving to Fentin, but he was determined not to show the white feather to his men.

Jayles turned to the soldiers and pointed to spots off each side of the road. "Set up the bows beside the road there, and there. Aim them toward the midpoint between those two houses," he said, pointing into Solemon, "and ready them to fire. We will attempt to lure the beast there." He looked at the men who had been called upon to goad the dragon into the crossbows' range. "Come with me. The moment of our testing is very near."

"You will lead them?" Fentin asked.

Jayles gave one grim nod. "One of us should. You stay here with the bowmen, and give the command to fire." He looked up at the steely sky; the afternoon was nearly spent. "We should go quickly."

Fentin looked into his comrade's eyes, and regretted that he did not have words sufficient to express the depth of his emotion. "God go with you," he said.

"And you, my friend."

Jayles and the six men who followed him crept quietly up the shadowed street, past shattered houses and the remains of broken warriors. They walked in a slight crouch, watching cautiously before, behind, around them, with their swords drawn and the breath shallow in their chests. They now doubted whether there would be a line of defenders to welcome them … they now feared that there might not be anyone at all.

Suddenly Jayles and his band of men froze in their tracks, hearts pounding in their chests. From back down the street where they had just come from, they heard the enraged roaring of what could only be the dragon, along with the faint sound of panicked shouts from the crossbow soldiers.

They heard a new sound then, which made their hearts quail—a whistling sound approaching overhead from the south. For a fraction of a second Jayles thought it was the dragon flying over Solemon, but then realized that one of the arrows from the crossbows had been launched. Jayles' men ducked and flinched, and the shaft passed directly over them, a wooden beam hurtling through the air.

It passed harmlessly between two ruined houses and landed with a thud in the open space between them, its metal tip embedding itself solidly in the earth, so that it looked for all the world like a new tree, freshly planted, but stripped of its branches and listing badly toward the south.

It took only a second to gather his wits and his courage. Jayles snapped, "Well, let's go," and ran back down the street toward the sounds of battle.

ŗ

While Sir Fentin had been pensively overseeing the placement and preparation of the crossbows, the dragon had been listening with placid curiosity. It had napped that afternoon in the feeble sunlight that fell on the open ground at the western end of Solemon, and the sounds of the approaching carts and horses had not particularly interested the beast, who at that moment preferred to draw some warmth from the sun's faint rays.

The dragon heard Jayles and the six who followed him begin making their way furtively toward the center of town, but did not thunder into the square to meet them. Instead, it crept with as much stealth as it could muster around the western perimeter of the town, where the voices of the men setting up the crossbows to the south could be heard. Engaged as they were with their work, the men did not see the approaching serpent until it was quite close—far too close to realign the bows.

Fentin was the first to notice the dragon, and he sounded a desperate cry of alarm. Without pausing to acknowledge his fear, he rushed toward his enemy, brandishing his sword, while the men behind him drew their own swords and their bows. As the first impotent volley of shafts pinged off the serpent's scaly hide, the beast turned and whipped its sinuous tail at Fentin, knocking him from his feet and sending him hurtling head-over-heels through the air to land in a broken heap against some low-lying shrubbery.

The dragon stomped toward the remaining soldiers, who were now scrambling behind the westernmost crossbow, trying to use it as a barrier between themselves and the huge reptile. The earth fairly trembled with the force of the beast's heavy tread as some of the bowmen tried to launch another volley. The dragon stepped across the oversized crossbow in order to reach the soldiers, and it inadvertently bumped against the weapon's release lever, which is what sent the metal-tipped shaft soaring over the heads of Jayles and his men in Solemon.

Startled by the firing of the bow, the serpent tipped its head back and roared indignantly, furiously. Two of the soldiers dropped their bows and covered their ears; another one shrieked, all thoughts of his own dignity abandoned.

The rest of the battle was not long. The dragon once again gorged on the blood and flesh of men, squashing the life from each one of the soldiers, either beneath its feet or within its jaws. The only one of the bowmen who escaped was one quavering man named Porcatie who stayed hidden, cowering beneath the cart that bore the easternmost crossbow.

Jayles and his band arrived at the end of the street, panting, just in time to see the dragon tossing the body of one of their companions high into the air and catching it, crunching it, crushing it. A quick scan of the battlefield revealed— could it be?—*nobody* left alive. And it had only been a few minutes!

Making a quick decision, Jayles shouted, "With me!" and once again began running back up the street toward the center of town. If any other defenders of Solemon remained, that's where they must be. Spying their movement out of the corner of its eye, the dragon turned and pursued them.

From his hiding place beneath the framework of the crossbow, Porcatie saw Jayles and his men appear briefly at the edge of town and then retreat. He also saw the dragon begin stumping up the King's Road after them, and made the most courageous decision he could make under the circumstances. Scrambling out from under the cart that sheltered him, he positioned himself at the firing mechanism of the crossbow, waited until the distance seemed right, then gave a sharp yank on the apparatus which was designed to release the shaft.

Nothing happened. Nothing, except the dragon kept on following the men toward the town.

Porcatie's duty with the crew had been to help load the weapon, and he had not been aware of just how hard he would have to heave on the lever in order to release the arrow.... Now his opportunity was gone.

Not knowing what else to do, Porcatie stared dumbly after the dragon for a long moment, watching it disappear up the streets of Solemon. Then he turned slowly and went to see if possibly Sir Fentin was still alive.

Chapter Five

Roarke rode Justice up a gently winding path that was familiar to him though he had not seen it in many years. Though the grass was now brown and the trees nearly bare, his mind's eye saw it as it had appeared in springtimes past: the trees covered with pink and white flowers, the creek burbling merrily alongside the path, the bleating of sheep in the distance. A place of beauty, simple beauty, country beauty ... but beauty nonetheless. Roarke wondered why he had wanted to leave.

He rode into the dooryard of the farmhouse and clambered down off his horse. The ground, which was always muddy here in the spring, was now hard and rutted with winter quickly approaching. He looked around at the little farm, remembering what was old, seeing what was new.

Clucking hens pecked the ground in front of a chicken coop that had been built recently, sometime after his last visit. Of course, that last visit was years ago now. He could hear the grunt of a pig from within the walls of the barn, which had been constructed on the same site as the other barn that used to be here, the one the dragon had destroyed so many years ago.

The door to the farmhouse swung quietly open, and a barefoot girl, maybe ten years old, maybe younger, stepped to the entrance.

"Whatcha doin'?" she asked Roarke.

"Hello, young lady," he replied. "I used to live here, long ago, and I just wanted to stop and see how your family was doing."

"Mama says I ain't supposed to come out."

"Your mama is correct," Roarke said. "What's your name?"

"Laini. What's yours?"

"Well, some of my very best friends call me Cedric, though I have some other names too. But you may call me Cedric if you wish."

"That's a nice name," she granted.

"Your name is very beautiful, too," Roarke said. "Is Eisen Parry your father?" Eisen Parry was the name of the man from Lauren that Roarke had sold his farm to, years ago, after he was awarded the title to Castle Thraill.

"No." The little girl's face contorted in puzzlement. "I think that was my grampa. He's dead."

Dead? Roarke thought sorrowfully. *How could that be? Why, he was only a few years older than me....* Then he remembered how old *he* was. Having a young wife and a young son ... had almost made him forget.

"Are you all alone here?" Roarke asked.

"No, I'm takin' care of my little sister. She's just a baby. Mama and Papa are out back, seein' if there's still apples worth pickin'." She scratched her head of tousled blonde hair, and Roarke wondered for a moment what Hollie had looked like when she was ten. Laini asked him, "Want to see my pig? His name's Bacon."

"Didn't your mother tell you that you had to stay in the house?"

"Oh, yeah." Laini frowned. "Well, you can go see him yourself, if you want to."

Roarke smiled at the little girl. "Maybe next time, if I come again someday."

"You can come again if you want to. Mama always likes people."

Roarke smiled, sighed, and took one last look around the barnyard. It seemed so much smaller than he had remembered it. He wondered why he had come ... but he didn't regret it. *Goodbye*, he said silently to his farm, his youth, his past ... he knew he would not be back.

He started to climb on Justice, and Laini said, "Where ya goin'?"

"I have something I need to do." He paused, one foot still in the stirrup.

"Don'tcha want to stay for supper?"

"That's very kind of you," he said. His sense of responsibility to fulfill Maygret's commission urged him on, but he also thought wistfully that he might like to spend a few more minutes talking to this nice young lady, and maybe eating a meal cooked by her mother. "Do you have lots of food?"

"No, not so much," she said, and grew somber. "Papa says we're gonna hafta butcher Bacon pretty soon."

"Well ... that should have happened a month ago, shouldn't it? Isn't fall the usual slaughtering time for pigs?"

"Yes, but I cried, and cried. And Papa said, 'Well, maybe we can wait for a bit at that.'"

Roarke felt for the little pouch of gold eglons that he had brought with him.

He didn't have very much gold with him on this trip, but he did have a few coins. "Do you love Bacon very much?"

"Oh, yes. He's my best friend. Except Mama."

"I'd like you to tell your father something for me. Do you think you can remember what I say?"

"I guess."

27

"I'm going to give you two coins. That should be enough to buy your family lots and lots of food."

"Okay," she said, and tentatively held out her hand.

"Tell your father that Cedric, Lord Roarke, came to your house today, and that with those two coins he purchased the pardon and deliverance of the noble pig Bacon. And that he gave said Bacon to the young woman named Laini, to keep Bacon safe and unharmed for Lord Roarke until such time as he should return and claim him."

Laini understood the general import what Roarke was saying, and a shy smile spread across her face, but she said, "I don't think I can remember all them words."

"That's all right," Roarke said, as he hoisted himself up on Justice's back. "Just tell him that the gold is for food, and that I want you to have Bacon."

"Thank you, Cedric." Laini did an imitation of the curtsey that her mother had been trying to teach her.

"You're a fine young lady, Laini." He slapped the reins gently against Justice's neck. "Goodbye."

"Goodbye, Cedric."

Chapter Six

Marta Dressler was a stout, middle-aged woman with two grown daughters and one small grandson. Once she had been slender and carefree, but then her husband Dan had died all too young, and she had become rather dour. Finding solace in food, she had mostly stopped coming out of her house, since almost every time she appeared at the Lord's table she had to commission a new, slightly larger gown.

She had squeezed herself into her latest dress this morning and hobbled uncomfortably up the lane to Castle Thraill, leaning heavily upon a wooden staff, to request an audience with the steward Esselte Smead, who was one of her oldest friends.

Smead welcomed her into his office. "Good morning, Marta! You're looking well."

"I look dreadful, and you know it, Esselte."

"Twaddle," Smead scoffed. "You look fine." They shared pleasantries for a few minutes, and then Smead asked, "To what do I owe the pleasure of your company this morning?"

"Thank you, Esselte," Marta began. "I don't want to make trouble."

"I'm sure of it. How may I help you?"

She decided to come directly to her point. "Cedric has gone off to fight the last dragon, I'm told."

Smead's face darkened, and he said uncomfortably, "Yes, it's true."

"I was wondering if he had made a change in his will."

"No ... there wasn't time."

"So, what does that mean for you and for me?"

Smead looked at her blankly for a moment. "Well ... I have hope that he will return."

"Of course." Marta wore a regretful expression on her round face. "Esselte, my friend, I really don't wish to cause trouble, and I understand that Dan's death has complicated matters ... but what will become of Cedric's estate that he promised you and Dan?"

"I have promised Lord Roarke that, should he fail to return from this battle, I will name his son Owan as my heir, which is as it should be."

"Yes. That's right." She looked as if she wanted to say more, but sat primly, awkwardly.

"What is it, Marta?"

"Well ... that's fine, for your half of the estate. You have no other heir. But what about my half?"

Smead stared at her for a moment, uncomprehending. "Your half?"

"It seems to me that, under the terms of Cedric's will, Dan's half of the treasury was to pass to his heirs. That would be me, the girls, and little Wylie."

"Yes, but Dan died ... before Cedric's will went into effect."

"Does that matter?" she asked sincerely.

"I ... I don't know," Smead admitted. He tried a different tack. "Haven't we treated you generously?"

"Of course. Magnificently." Marta reached out and took Smead's hand, imploring him to understand. "Esselte, you can give us a life of wealth, of security, of unbounded comfort. I admit this, and I am appreciative of it. But I don't want my grandson to grow up as a spoiled, pampered, ungrateful whelp."

She continued, "What Cedric promised Dan was not the privilege of wealth. It was the chance for ... greatness."

She released Smead's hand, and sighed, her large bosom rising and falling with the passage of her breath. "I don't ask for you to make little Wylie a rich man. I am asking for you to grant him the opportunity to serve his people, to learn to care for them like Cedric does—like you do. To be, perhaps ... a Lord."

"I see." Smead thought for several minutes, wondering how to handle this situation, while Marta Dressler waited patiently. "What if you have more grandsons someday?"

"I don't recall that being an issue when Cedric sent his will to the king."

"No, I suppose not." He thought again for a few moments. "Marta, this is a difficult question."

"I know. I'm sorry. But what kind of grandmother would I be, if I hadn't at least asked?"

"Indeed. Well," he decided, "when Lord Roarke returns to Thraill, we must have him clarify his will. I expect he will just name Owan as his heir."

"Of course."

"And if he doesn't return—God forbid—then I suppose we must ask the king himself for his judgment."

"I pray it doesn't come to that," Marta said earnestly, and Smead was impressed with her sincerity.

"As do I."

꠸

Will had been gone from Castle Thraill for longer than he had planned, and Piper was dreadfully worried for him. These were the most terrifying days she had ever known in her life, chiefly because of the dragon's attack on Solemon and her Uncle Cedric's lamentable departure. But her fiancé was unaccounted for, gone away to the wild northern wastes, and it was that fact which consumed her with dread. She was quiet, pensive, distracted, like a fretful wraith, a silent shadow haunting the halls of Thraill.

She had not been to see Aunt Hollie since Uncle Cedric had left for the battlefield. She knew that Hollie was probably frightened and alone, just as Piper was, but she was ashamed to admit how sad and desperate she felt, to someone who probably had far more tangible reasons to feel sad and desperate.

She made up her mind to visit Hollie today. If Piper didn't go to Hollie to offer comfort and commiseration, then who would? Her mother?

꠸

Jesi Tenet sat on her Aunt Hollie's window seat, cradling her cousin Owan in her arms, softly singing a lullaby that her mother used to sing to her when she was a baby. Hollie was sitting at her desk, trying to sketch pictures of the small flowers she had picked in the wilderness when she had traveled from Blythecairne to Thraill with Cedric and Willum. It seemed so long ago now. But it cheered her heart to remember beautiful things and happy times. Picnics on the grass and flowers in her hair and a noble husband smiling up at her from where he lay drowsing.

Jesi came to the end of her song and stopped. Hollie asked, "Do you have another song? I very much enjoy listening to you sing."

"I don't know any other ones that would be good for Owan.... I could sing that one again."

"Please."

She began again in a high, sweet voice:

> *Sleep, little baby, sleep—*
> *safe in the arms that love you.*
> *Dream, little baby, dream—*
> *nothing can harm you now.*
>
> *Everything in the world's alright—*
> *nothing to spoil your dreams tonight.*
> *Sleep in these arms 'til the morning light—*
> *'til morning brightly comes.*
>
> *Sleep, little baby, sleep—*
> *safe in the arms that love you.*
> *Dream, little baby, dream—*
> *nothing can harm you now.*

Piper had arrived at the door to Hollie's room and listened to her sister softly singing, and had experienced a pang of guilt that she—Piper—was not the one singing a lullaby to Owan. Then she thought repentantly that it was better that Hollie had Jesi than no one at all, and was about to turn and go when her aunt spied her standing in the doorway.

"Piper," she beckoned. "I've missed you."

Piper entered the room, gave Hollie a long hug, sniffled, and said, "I'm sorry. I've been missing Will so much, and I didn't want to sound selfish and insensitive."

"A little selfishness between friends is all right. We need to stick together, we women who are waiting for our men to come home."

Jesi felt a little bit hurt then, a little left out. She wasn't waiting for anyone to come home. But Hollie said to Piper, "Your sister has been keeping me good company, helping with the baby and keeping my spirits up. She has been a treasure." Jesi smiled faintly, and kissed Owan's velvety forehead.

Chapter Seven

Roarke camped for the evening beside the Strait Penne. Tomorrow he would leave the King's Road and pick his way over the Sayl Mountains, and then ride hard across the open plain until he came to the central forest of Greening, where the Eldric River flowed. Assuming he arrived at the forest somewhere near the headwaters of the Eldric, it should be only a few more days of riding due east, and he should be in the streets of Solemon. Perhaps he wasn't riding quite as swiftly as Queen Maygret's commission directed ... but if this was to be his last journey across Hagenspan, he thought he might as well savor it. Besides, it wouldn't do any good for him to arrive at the battlefield exhausted.

His dinner was sizzling in the pan and water being boiled for tea when he heard a voice hail him from the edge of the King's Road. "Ho, the camp! Might I approach?"

"Yes, and welcome," Roarke said. "You may share my meal if you wish. It's just biscuit and vegetables."

"Well, I don't come empty-handed," Sir Keltur said, as he stepped into the light cast by the campfire, bearing two squirrels that he had brought down with his bow.

"Keltur! I thought you had gone back to Ruric's Keep."

"I had. But I turned around."

"You are most welcome," Roarke said, reaching out to grasp his hand.

Then, thinking that perhaps he had misunderstood Keltur's intention, he asked, "Where are you headed?"

"Here. Right here. If you will permit me to accompany you to the battleground, I may be of some small use to you."

"Thank you," Roarke accepted, though he was a little reluctant. "In the past, I have always met the serpents on my own, and I believe the Almighty has favored me because of my dependence upon Him, Him alone. Is that acceptable to you?"

"Yes. I'm here just to serve you, Sir Roarke, in any way that I can. I don't desire glory or reward for myself. Just to save face before the king and the knights, for I believe I have lost their favor."

Roarke studied his companion's rugged face. "How could you have lost favor?"

"Just a feeling I have." He began preparing the squirrels for the pan. "King Ruric had some new weapons built, and sent a troop to Solemon, hoping to win the day. He placed Sir Fentin and Sir Jayles in charge, both of them fine fighting men, to be sure." He looked at Roarke. "That should have been my command."

The sounds and smells of searing meat filled the campsite, as Keltur continued his story. "I believe the king sensed reluctance on my part to go and face the dragon. It was real, of course—I hadn't the heart to go. In fact, I even suggested to the king that he should ask *you* to go and fight. I believe my suggestion was interpreted as cowardice. And perhaps that's what it was.

"I didn't want to die," he said, almost to himself. "Of course I didn't. But now I find ... that I am already dead. For what is a knight without honor? What is a man without respect?" Answering his own question, he said softly, "Nothing. I must have honor in order to live. I must have it."

Keltur shook the frying pan, turning the meat over. "When Queen Maygret prepared her commission, Ruric Serpent's-Bane chose me to deliver it to you. A task worthy of a common messenger-boy. Not the captain of the king's guard."

Roarke said placatingly, "Perhaps he meant to honor me by sending you with the queen's commission."

Keltur grunted. "Perhaps."

The two men sat silently for awhile then, eating their dinner, drinking tea with a dollop of something from a flask Keltur carried. As dusk began to settle around them, Roarke said cautiously, "I do not wish to offend you, my friend … but if you have bitterness in your heart, I must ask that you let me ride on without you."

"No, Sir Roarke, I have no bitterness. I only said what I said so that you would understand my intentions. My motivation."

"Very well." Roarke looked at the other knight in the glowing light cast by the waning embers of the fire. "Very well." A snowflake appeared out of the darkness, glistening fairy-white in the firelight, and then another one. "Are you a praying man, Keltur?"

"Sometimes."

"That's good. We will have need of each other's prayers before this adventure is done."

Chapter Eight

The dragon had killed three of Jayles' six men before they had been able to escape to shelter, apprehending them from behind and snatching them from their feet, tossing them high into the air and catching them. Jayles heard the outraged cries of his comrades as they flew, startled, terrified, far above the ground, and he heard when their cries were suddenly stifled with the sound of a crack or a crunch. Then he heard, felt, the thundering of the dragon's tread as it pursued again.

Jayles and the remaining three stumbled into the dusty town square, quickly registering the fact that this was a scene of such devastation as they had never before imagined: storefronts shattered, the street dug up, trees and greenery uprooted. Jayles shouted to the others, "Take cover! I'm making a stand!"

One of the men whose job it had been to lure the dragon before the bow— his name was Creighton—cried, "I'll stand with you," and drew his sword. Another, named Preston, said, "And I." The last man, Hauer, said nothing, but swallowed nervously and drew his blade. The four stood their ground in a small arc, facing the serpent, which approached them slowly now, warily, a rumbling growl shaking the air.

Jayles was about to step toward the beast and utter a shout of defiance, when a movement on his periphery captured his attention. From about the same level as the dragon's head, a figure rose, and Jayles perceived that it was from a nearby rooftop. Turning to take a quick glance at what it might be, he was gratified to note that it was a man with a bow. *So there are some left after all!* Silently the man on the roof loosed his shaft, which sped through the air unswervingly toward the dragon's head. The arrow would have struck the dragon directly in its right eye if the beast had not also been alerted by the slight movement that it sensed. But it turned its head slightly toward the motion, and the arrow glanced off its snout and landed in the street. While the attack did nothing to harm the beast, it did serve to distract it, to enrage it. Turning its massive body and taking an angry step toward the building where the man stood, the dragon tilted its head back and emitted a wrathful howl.

"Now!" cried the man on the rooftop. "Get inside! Run!"

Jayles, comprehending the prudence of that command, made a quick motion to his men, and they scrambled toward the building where the man was. "Go!" he hissed.

The dragon, whose attention had been momentarily diverted by the man on the roof, realized that its prey was escaping, and charged after them.

Another young man emerged from the shattered door of the structure, beckoning feverishly to the four soldiers. "This way!" Creighton and Hauer reached the doorway, tumbling through, and Jayles was close behind them. Pausing at the doorway to see whether Preston would make it, Jayles cried, "Come *on*!" He reached out and grabbed Preston by the shirt, and hurled him forcefully through the entryway. As he did so, he lost his balance, and was surprised to find himself suddenly flying through the air, high into the sky.

Jayles almost laughed. The world looked so different from up here! Everything was so small, and he could see it all at once: the town square, the buildings, the streets beyond the square, the dragon waiting below. This must be what the vision of God was like! It was exhilarating.

Then he began to descend, and was sorry to think that he would never be able to tell anybody about his experience.

"Welcome to Bedford's Tap—our stronghold," said the man who had held the door open for the soldiers. "I expect it's a bitter pill fer you boys to swaller, but ye're part an' parcel with us now. I welcome ye t' the Defenders o' Solemon."

Creighton said angrily, tearfully, "Are you *jesting*? Our leader and our friends have just been killed!"

"Easy, now," the youth warned. "The dragon kilt my own best friend, an' it also kilt the best friend o' the feller on the rooftop what just saved yer bacon. We ain't no strangers t' loss." His voice softened. "I expect we can give ye a few minutes t' moan an' cry. But pretty soon, ye're goin' t' hafta decide what ye're goin' t' do. Ye can just wither up an' die, or ye can join the fight. We might not make too much of a difference in the battle in the end, but whatever difference we can make, we will."

Creighton, Hauer, and Preston knelt on their hands and knees on the floor of the shop where they had found refuge, panting, tears of exhaustion and loss coursing down their cheeks into their beards. After a few moments of dark, confused sorrow, Creighton said, "Forgive me."

"Not at all, friend. We have a little water, if ye'd like a sip."

"I will, if I may," Preston said softly. The young Defender of Solemon fetched a skin of water and gave it to Preston, who took a swallow, and then passed the skin to Hauer, who did likewise and gave it to Creighton.

"Who's your captain?" Creighton asked. They could still hear the dragon raging and stomping around in the square.

"Well, unless one o' ye fellers can trump the last remainin' soldier who actually came from Solemon, it's him. His name's Casterline, an' he's off tryin' t' find us some grub. There ain't much."

Handing the skin of water back, Creighton said, "We will join you, of course. Our own captain was Sir Jayles of Ruric's Keep, who...." He nodded back toward the street.

"Who gave his life for me," Preston said sadly.

"Are ye fellers all knights?"

"No, just common soldiers. It was our task to lure the dragon within range of the king's crossbows."

"The dragon has a way o' spoilin' our plans, don't it?"

Creighton looked at him grimly. "My name's Creighton, and this is Hauer, and Preston from Raussi."

"Pleased as could be t' meet ye. I'm Tinker, of Yancey's Brigade from Castle Blythecairne, though it's long odds whether I'll ever see that fair land again." He held out his hand. "Padallor from Katarin is on the roof. He's a stouthearted lad— ye'll like 'im. Casterline from Solemon should be back before dark, if the dragon don't get 'im. There's only one more of us, an' he's one o' the king's knights, like you. He's in the back room there. Name's Sir Tellis ... but I fear he's just aboot used up."

"I know Tellis," Hauer said, and went to the back room to see what could be done for him.

"Do you boys have a plan?" Preston asked Tinker.

"Not much o' one," he admitted. "Just hold on an' look out fer our opportunity. Paddy up on the roof has been tryin' t' shoot out the dragon's eye ever since he got here. That seems like as good of an idear as any of 'em."

Preston thought of something and turned to Creighton. "I'll bet one of the crossbows is still loaded and ready to fire."

Creighton's bushy eyebrows rose in surprise. "You may be right...."

"And even if it's not loaded, the arrows must still be there, so it could be loaded again, as long as the dragon hasn't busted up the crossbows."

"What're these bows ye're talkin' aboot?" Tinker asked, and the two soldiers explained about King Ruric's weapons.

"Well, that sounds hopeful," Tinker said. "I don't s'pose there's any food down there too?"

"Yes ... but it's kind of out in the open, now. I don't know if it's worth the risk to try to get it back."

"It is," Tinker said matter-of-factly. "When ye're as hungry as we been ... it's worth it." He shouted loudly, presumably up to the roof. "Paddy! Come on down!" They could hear a thumping above the ceiling, indicating that Paddy had heard. "You boys got any other good news?"

Creighton, who wasn't sure whether Tinker was still poking fun at him, said tentatively, "Perhaps.... At the same time that King Ruric sent us north with his crossbows, he sent Keltur to Castle Thraill with the queen's commission. The king was hopeful that it wouldn't be necessary ... but I believe Sir Roarke is coming."

Paddy was coming through the door from the back room just then, and he said, "What's that?"

Tinker looked at him with new hope in his eyes. "Hear that, Paddy? Roarke's comin'!!"

"Well, what do you know about that? We might just get saved after all."

Chapter Nine

Sir Keltur pointed eastward to where a thready column of smoke rose from the northern edge of the forest. Roarke, who had also seen the smoke, nodded.

"It's nearly time to camp anyway. Shall we make for the fire?" Keltur asked.

Roarke nodded again. The sun, which was setting behind their backs, cast long shadows before them; it was as if the marks of their own passage were preceding them across the plain. Roarke said, "It'll be brisk tonight; a fire will be welcome."

"Who do you suppose it is? Refugees from Solemon?"

"We'll know soon."

The two rode on in a wary silence until they reached the place where the scattered low-lying bushes of the plain began growing closer, thicker, taller. Soon they were at the edge of the forest itself, and then they needed to pick their way slowly through the woods to the place they figured the fire might be, since the column of smoke was now obscured by the thickness of the trees.

Keltur touched Roarke's arm and pointed. Visible in what looked to be a small clearing between the trees were the dancing lights cast by a campfire. Two horses were picketed there, and one man bent over the flames, preparing food.

Roarke looked at Keltur and nodded. Keltur then rode forward, calling, "Ho, the camp! May I enter?"

The man at the fire—only a boy, actually—jumped, frightened, but he said, "Yes, you may enter."

Keltur stepped his horse into the clearing, and said, "I have a companion. We would share your camp tonight, if you have no objection."

"No, that's alright," the boy said nervously.

Keltur turned and nodded toward the shadowy perimeter of the camp, and Roarke stepped from the darkness, holding the reins of his black stallion Justice, who appeared almost invisible in the murky dusk.

"Why, it's Lord Roarke!" said Brette with relief.

"You're Poppleton's squire, are you not?" Roarke asked. "Where's your— Where is Alan?" (Roarke had almost asked, "Where's your master?" but feared that he might offend the young squire by referring to Alan as his master.)

"Right here, Lord Roarke," said Alan Poppleton, stepping from the shadows behind him with his sword drawn. "We heard you coming, and thought it best to take precautions. We didn't know it was you, of course."

"Well done." Roarke reached out and gave Alan's shoulder a pat. "You look as if you've been unwell."

"I have. I was as weak as a kitten for about a week, and Brette nursed me back to health. I'd hate to think where I'd have been without him."

Brette blushed, pleased with the acknowledgement. "It was nothing."

Keltur nodded grimly. "Not such a little thing. My life has been preserved by a worthy squire more than once."

"As has mine," Roarke agreed.

"I am Keltur, from Ruric's Keep," Keltur said, reaching out to grasp Brette's hand.

"Brette, ah, from Ester."

"Well met. And you—" Keltur said, turning to Alan, "you must be the son of Poppleton, Lord of Ester."

"Yes, sir. I am honored to know you."

"Have you food enough for all of us?" Roarke asked. "We have some jerky and cold biscuits we could contribute."

"Thank you, my Lord, but that won't be necessary," Brette said. "Alan shot us a fine tender hart just today, which I was just fixing to fry." Reconsidering, he said, "Well, we could use the biscuits, if you like."

Sir Fentin's eyes fluttered, and Porcatie breathed a prayer of thanks. He had dragged Fentin into the brush near where the knight had landed after being swept from the earth by the dragon's tail. Now he cradled Fentin's head in his lap, the brush serving as a woven canopy just above them. Some of the knight's bones were clearly broken: an arm, a leg, and who knew what else? Porcatie didn't know what to do to help him now … except to keep him undiscovered by the dragon.

"Porcatie? Is that you?" Fentin whispered.

"Yes, Sir Fentin."

"Apparently I am not dead."

"No."

"And neither are you…. Have we won the day?"

Porcatie paused a moment before answering. "No, Sir Fentin."

A painful sigh escaped Fentin's lips, and he grimaced. "Where are the others?" he asked.

"I, ah, I don't, ah, believe there *are* any."

"Good God," Fentin whispered.

"Yes. No," Porcatie agreed sadly.

Fentin lapsed back into unconsciousness then, and sometime before the breaking of the day, he breathed his last breath. When Porcatie woke in the coldness of dawn, his back stiff and complaining, he realized that Fentin, whose head was still in his lap, was dead, and he wept, as silently as he could.

Brette had said very little while the four men shared their supper, for he was afraid that if he spoke, he might show himself to be a fool. But he was very glad that the two knights had arrived; they offered him a sense of security that had been starting to melt like snow on the frying pan, at least for Brette. As he had tended his friend during his weeklong illness, he had realized that if he could whip Alan right now—which he certainly could—what good would Alan be against a *dragon*, for God's sake? And then, what would happen to Brette?

Alan had also been relieved to see Lord Roarke once again. And Sir Keltur seemed to be a formidable ally as well. The two knights had discussed their plans for the coming days, with Alan and Brette listening politely, Alan occasionally asking questions or making small comments.

Roarke figured that two more days of steady riding would put them squarely in Solemon. He made it clear that, because he bore the queen's commission, the burden of battle was his to bear—that is, if the dragon had not been already subdued by the king's crossbows. "If I fall, though ... then it will be up to the three of you to decide what you must do next."

Alan said, "I confess, I am comforted to think that you will be going before me, and that I may not need to face the serpent at all. But, Lord Roarke ... if *you* should fall ... then whatever will anyone *else* be able to do?"

Roarke and Keltur looked at each other soberly. Roarke said slowly, "We must *believe*. We must believe that God's purposes for Hagenspan ... are not to see it utterly destroyed. Even though He has allowed us to be humbled by the dragon for a season ... must He not rather desire life instead of death ... love instead of hate? Ultimately ... must He not?

"If I fall, then the Almighty will raise up another deliverer. If the responsibility for this fight—if this burden, this doom, becomes yours to bear—if it does, then you must pray. Cast yourself upon the providence of the Almighty."

He exhaled heavily and said in a grim voice, "God will provide. May it be sooner rather than later. May it be that each one of us lives to kiss our loved ones again. And if not ... if not ... God will provide."

Chapter Ten

King of the Dragon complained, "I'm gettin' powerful hungry." Tilda and Vesta, the kobolds, had absconded with not only the two packhorses, but also all of the gear and supplies that the horses bore. On the trip southward to Thraill, food had been only what Will could bring down with his bow, and that had not been much.

"We'll eat tonight, I'll promise ye," Will said. "We're almost there."

The rolling hills of Haioland were brown now, and the higher elevations had dustings of snow. But Will was glad to be back among surroundings that he could recognize as being home, and his horse Starlight also seemed to know that he was close to a dry stable and oats.

"Today, then?" the King asked anxiously.

"Aye. Do ye want to ride right in with me, or do you want me to go in by myself first and then come back for ye?"

"I'll go right in wi' ye, if'n ye don't mind. It'll be skeery ... but not so much as bein' left alone in this odd grassy place."

For Will, the return to the grasslands had been a warming, welcoming occasion. But he realized that the King had been living among the rocks and boulders and caves for such a long time that what was welcoming to Will was foreign and fretful to the little kobold. He said, "I think ye'll like the castle. It's all made of stone."

"Yes, that sounds cozy," the King said doubtfully.

Γ

Piper sat in the garden, which was a tangle of brown vines and paper-dry leaves. She looked up at the stone dragon, water still dribbling from its mouth, and silently cursed it. Her mother had ordered the construction of the fountain with the idea that a dragon would honor Uncle Cedric, and it was true that all of the good things Piper had known during her life had been an indirect result of Roarke's conflict with that first dragon at Lauren. But now ... the dragon had come to symbolize all that was troubling and helpless in Piper's life.

Some of the men, the soldiers and guards of Castle Thraill, had gone off to the battle for Solemon in response to the petition from Sir Tellis, and they had not been heard from again. Those men were Piper's friends. They were like big brothers to her, protective and doting. Uncle Cedric himself was now gone, too, of course, and Piper was forlorn without him ... it seemed like such a short time since he had come home with Aunt Hollie ... now, would he ever come home again?

But what worried her most was Willum. He had not gone to fight the dragon—no, not yet. But he was gone, somewhere, and Piper was lonely and despondent. And someday, if he came home, someday, maybe he would have to go and fight the dragon too. Then, what would happen to Piper? How would her heart ever be unbroken? Where would the babies come from that she now longed to fill her arms with—the babies with big brown eyes and quick little crooked smiles?

She took a handful of graying leaves and crushed them in her fist, scattering the crumbled bits in the fountain's rippling pool. She watched the bits of leaf follow their implacable paths as they were compelled toward the place where the water spattered from the dragon's mouth into the pool, causing the crumbs to be submerged and lost from her sight.

"There you are!" her sister said, practically dancing into the garden.

"Hello, Jesi," Piper said morosely. She was glad to see her sister, but could not summon a smile. She dusted the clinging bits of leaf from her hands.

Jesi simply said, "He's here."

Piper's head snapped up, and she asked, "Will?"

Jesi smiled and nodded. "Will's here."

Piper leaped from the fountain and raced past her sister toward the courtyard. Jesi watched Piper run, then smiled again, and followed.

ʳ

Will stood in the courtyard next to Starlight, and he also held the reins to another horse, upon which King of the Dragon sat trembling. Esselte Smead strode happily toward them, having been notified by the guard on duty that Sir Willum had returned.

King of the Dragon was claustrophobic; he felt that he had made a terrible mistake by allowing himself to be led within these imposing walls, even though he felt that he could trust Willum. Mostly.

Now he saw Smead coming toward them—Smead, who was by far the largest human that the King had ever seen—and he felt weak and vulnerable. Remembering Vesta's impressive ruse from the northlands, he said in faint voice, "Bats!"

Will chuckled and said, "Don't fear, Yer Majesty. This feller is a friend, a good one."

"Arright ... because ye say so."

Smead stepped to Will and threw his arms around him. "Sir Willum! You have been greatly missed!"

"Thank you, Master Smead. It's good to be home again," Will said, returning the embrace.

"You have been greatly missed," Smead repeated.

"May I present to ye my friend? Esselte Smead, this is the King o' the Dragon."

"Welcome! I say … you wouldn't be a kobold, would you?"

"So I hear," said the King.

"Well, this is outstanding! I've never met one of your people before." Smead reached up a hand to greet the little creature, and King of the Dragon tentatively grasped his fingers. "My grandfather used to know of your people, long ago near the Sayl Mountains. But he told me your eyes were colored red, not yellow."

"I've seen his eyes get kind of orangey when he gets excited," offered Will.

"Outstanding," murmured Smead distractedly.

At that moment, Piper came dashing from the garden and rushed into Will's welcoming arms. Tears welled up in her eyes as she struggled to hold back her sobs, and she clung to Will, demanding, "Don't ever leave me again."

Will smiled over the top of Piper's head apologetically to Smead, and he said, "Would ye please tell Lord Roarke that I've come back?"

"Yes. Well," Smead said uncomfortably, "Lord Roarke is not here at the castle just now."

"Really? Where has he gone?"

"We'll talk after a bit. First, you take some time and let Miss Paipaerria welcome you home."

With a surprised little start, Piper noticed King of the Dragon peering at her curiously from astride the horse. "Don't be skeered," the King said comfortingly.

"Are you King of the Dragon?" she asked, though she realized instantly that it could scarcely be anyone else.

"Aye, that's what I'm called," he said, with a glance toward Willum. "An' ye must be Sir Willum's Piper."

"I am honored to meet you, Your Majesty. Please forgive my tears."

"That's arright," the King said. He continued in a confidential tone, "Ye know ... I b'lieve Sir Willum likes you even more'n he likes *me*."

His arms still around Piper, Will watched Smead walking slowly back into the castle and wondered uneasily where Roarke had gone.

Chapter Eleven

The dragon was becoming increasingly drowsy. She had glutted freely for many days on the blood of all of the little morsels that had presented themselves to her—willing sacrifices—and she was nearly ready to begin preparing the nest that would be her bed for the next slumbering century.

But there was still something left undone ... until it was accomplished, the four snarling demons that indwelt her would not permit her to rest. This annoyed the serpent terribly ... but all she could do was obey, no matter how she tried to resist. She tried stomping, she tried biting, but nothing worked. Nothing could make the silent voices of command deep within her stop their incessant, insistent meddling.

She was looking for something ... *they* were looking for something. She didn't know what. They would let her know when she found it, though. Whatever it was, she wanted to find it soon, because she was growing weary, weary of chasing the little gnat-like men that came and bothered her with their sticks and stones ... even though they *were* delicious.

Thinking of their lip-smacking tastiness caused the dragon to remember the little band of humans that she had not yet been able to reach, back in the hidden center of the wooden buildings. There was one man in particular ... the one on the top of the roof. She had seen him before, on the plain between her stone fortress and this village of wood, and had wanted to eat him then, but the compulsion inside her would not allow it. Now the little creature—instead of appreciating the mercy she had shown him—hid like a roach just out of reach on the top of the building, and kept on popping up and shooting stinging little darts at her face. She growled, a low, throaty rumble.

Maybe that's what she was looking for. She paused, only partly finished with uprooting a large tree whose branches annoyed her for some reason, and stealthily crept back to the center of town.

༄

In Bedford's Tap the seven Defenders of Solemon sat in a circle on teetering chairs and edges of tables, in the mottled light that filtered between the cracks of boarded-up windows, and made such plans as they could. Since Sir Tellis showed some signs of recovering from his injuries, the question of leadership had arisen again, with Creighton, Hauer, and Preston thinking that one of King Ruric's knights should probably be the one who gave the commands.

But Tellis, whose pains were as much emotional as they were physical, said quietly, "I don't want to lead."

Casterline said, "I'd be willing to follow Paddy. He's got as much sand as any of us here."

Tinker offered, "Aye. An' it was Paddy what saw the dragon first an' lived, out of all of us here anyways."

Paddy shook his head. "I think you've been doin' just fine," he said, looking at Casterline. "There's no need to change."

No one had anything to say to that, so it's likely that the men would have given Casterline a vote of confidence, except that the moment was violently interrupted.

Crashing through the boards of the window in an explosion of splintered wood and shards of glass came the head of the dragon, who had moved with marvelous stealth to the front of Bedford's Tap, and stood listening to the voices of the men inside. When it heard Paddy's voice, it recognized him from the defiant cries he sometimes made from the rooftop.

Even though the dull-witted beast could scarcely discern the difference between the solid wall of the building and the boarded-up window, the serpent chose to bash its head through the wooden planks anyway, toward the place Paddy's voice came from.

The dragon could only reach halfway into the room—its shoulders nearly became wedged in the wall. But that was far enough that it was able to snap Casterline, Tinker, and Preston up in one great bite, dragging them from the building, their legs hanging from the serpent's jaws, their feet involuntarily jerking in a morbid dance.

The remaining four scrambled from the front room and escaped out the back of the building, slipping into the store next door and diving to the floor, where they lay silently, their hearts pounding and their eyes wide with terror.

On the street in front of Bedford's Tap, the dragon tried to toss its three men into the air and catch them, but when it did so, the men flew off in three different directions instead of going uniformly straight up in the air, and when the dragon tried to catch all of them at once, it missed them altogether.

Preston was dead when his body hit the dusty square; he had been clamped directly between the dragon's teeth when he was dragged from the building. Casterline landed on the cold, hard street, still alive, but he was unable to move; his brain told his body to stand and run, but nothing in his body was able to respond.

Tinker bounced off the street, bleeding and broken, but somehow scrambled to his feet and ran for the narrow crack between Bedford's Tap and the building next door, the one where his friends had fled. Wedging his way between the buildings, just out of reach of the pursuing serpent, he had the sudden thought that it probably would have been better for him to stay and let the dragon kill him, instead of painfully cramming himself someplace where he would never depart, where he would just bleed to death. Soon, if he was lucky.

The four men lying on the floor heard the dragon bashing its head against the two storefronts trying to reach Tinker. Dust and bits of ceiling fell down, drifting through the room's murky air, and rested on their heads. Paddy, who lay facing Tellis, looked into his eyes grimly and said nothing.

Battering its head against the corners of the buildings was quickly painful, even for the dragon, so it turned angrily away and snapped up Casterline and Preston, crunching, growling, swallowing, then bellowing.

The four men on the floor heard the roar, then felt the boards shake beneath them as the dragon stomped back away out of town once again. They stayed where they were, facedown in the dust. After awhile they heard Tinker, moaning sorrowfully from his spot wedged between the buildings. A few minutes later, they heard the moans become words, faintly discernible from the other side of the wall, as Tinker prayed to God.

"I guess I'm comin' to meet Ye now, Yer Lordship," he groaned. "I don't mean no disrespect ... but I sure hope Yer country is better than *this* one turned out t' be."

Paddy looked again into the helpless, desperate orbs of Sir Tellis. Then he closed his own eyes, and dreamed about what he would tell Sarie when he got home, imagining her face before him—wondering, awe-filled, proud of her husband, a little bit cross with him—until he fell asleep, wearing a faint smile upon his lips.

The dragon was not sure if she had gotten the man she was trying to get— they all tasted about the same. But her immediate appetite had been sated ...and there was still that vexing tree to finish tearing from the earth.

Chapter Twelve

Porcatie wasn't sure where to go. He was pretty sure that he didn't want to go back to Ruric's Keep and report the failure of the mission to the king. He had the uneasy feeling that Ruric and his remaining knights would wonder why Porcatie wasn't killed with the rest of the men. So he didn't really want to take the road south, which led directly back to Ruric's Keep—besides which, he would be very exposed and vulnerable.

If he chose to go either east or north, that would mean he would have to go right past Solemon and the dragon, so that was out. That only left the west....

Porcatie remembered the smoke rising from the forest that he had seen in the west when he was on his way to the battle for Solemon with Fentin and Jayles.

Maybe there *were* refugees there, who had fled from the approaching serpent. Maybe he would find sanctuary with them ... understanding ... a chance to start over. Maybe he would even find some courage there ... he imagined himself leading a band of refugees back to Solemon to fight for its deliverance.... No, that was probably too much to expect.

He waited until he was pretty certain the dragon had gone back to the center of Solemon, then crept out from underneath the brush, where flies buzzed around Sir Fentin's sleeping corpse. Crouching low to the ground, he looked carefully in every direction, and, seeing no sign of the serpent, he stood and started walking toward the razor-thin line on the western horizon that was all he could see of the distant forest.

Roarke and Keltur rode toward the sunset, with Alan and Brette behind them. Tomorrow morning, Roarke thought, tomorrow morning he would be in Solemon and facing the dragon. The men rode calmly, quietly, pensively. There was not really anything that needed to be said.

As they were drawing near the outskirts of the little town nestled in the low-lying foothills of the Senn Mountains, they could see the silhouette of the king's crossbows in the distance. Roarke looked at Keltur, who said, "Yes, those are the king's weapons." He peered at the structures through the dusk. "It appears as if only one of them has been fired." A thrill of hope fluttered in Keltur's chest.

"Maybe it worked!" he said softly. "Maybe they got the dragon."

Brette interrupted their hopeful thoughts with an urgent, "Lord Roarke!" He pointed northward. "Look!"

A man was running toward them. Where he was coming from, and why he was on foot so far away from town was curious … but it probably wasn't good.

The four horsemen changed their course and rode up to meet him.

"I know you," Sir Keltur said to the bedraggled man, who had stopped, panting, his hands on his knees.

"Porcatie, sir."

"Yes, of course. Weren't you … weren't you with Jayles and Fentin?" Keltur asked uneasily.

"Yes."

Roarke asked, hoping against hope, "Did you prevail?"

Porcatie did not recognize Roarke—they had never met—but he knew that that was who the white-haired knight had to be. He said, "My Lord, I'm sorry, but no!" He shook his head. "No!"

Keltur asked severely, "The others? Are there dead?"

Porcatie nodded sadly.

"How many? Are Fentin and Jayles all right?"

Porcatie shook his head. "Jayles, maybe, but not Fentin."

"Speak clearly, Porcatie," Keltur said desperately. "How many of you are left?"

"It's possible that there could be as many as seven, sir. But I only know for sure about one. Me."

Roarke interrupted, "Have you wounded the dragon?"

"Oh, no, my Lord, I surely don't think so."

Roarke turned his horse back toward the west, and stared toward the sunset as if he could see all the way to Castle Thraill. "Damn."

ʕ

The five men made a cold camp right where they were, and Porcatie told them of all that had transpired in Solemon since he had arrived—at least, all the things that he had knowledge of, which was not very much.

Roarke said to his comrades, "I have an important engagement tomorrow morning, so I will have to cut short my participation in this conversation, regretfully. The only news about Solemon that I really need to know right now is that the dragon is still alive, and that has been confirmed."

"I'm sorry, my Lord," said Porcatie.

Roarke smiled at him.

"There is something I need to do before I take my rest. Alan," he said to Poppleton, "can you write?"

"Of course," Alan said, surprised.

"Do you have something to write on?"

"I believe we do," said Brette, and got the materials out of a saddle pack.

"I beg your indulgence," Roarke said to them all, "but I would like to dictate two letters—one to my wife, and one to my son—to be delivered in the event that I do not survive the battle."

Keltur nodded, and the others waited respectfully to hear what he would say.

"First, to Owan ... are you ready?" he asked Alan, who nodded affirmatively. "To Owan Roarke, my son ... the greatest regret of my life ... is the fact that I was not able to spend more time with you." He waited for Alan to catch up. "But I just want you to know ... that in the moments we spent together ... you were loved, my boy.... Listen to your mother ... and Master Smead ... and wear your name proudly.... I will be watching you ... and waiting for you ... in God's country."

"Is that all?" asked Alan as he finished writing, and regretted his choice of words.

"Yes, that should do it. Hand it here and let me sign it." Roarke dipped the quill in Brette's ink bottle and signed the piece of parchment with a flourish, and said, "Now for Hollie's."

Handing the pen back to Alan, he began. "To Hollie Roarke, my beloved ... my greatly beloved.... Knowing and loving you ... has been the greatest honor a man could ever have.... Thank you...." He paused a moment, trying to formulate a thought that would be meaningful to Hollie. "I thank God ... that He allowed us these glorious days.... Even though I shall not see you again ... trust His goodness."

He looked at Keltur and said ruefully, "That wasn't very good, was it?"

"She will treasure your words, my Lord."

Roarke smiled sadly, and said, "I pray she will never have to read them." He held out his hand to Alan, who passed him the letter. He signed it, "With all my love, Cedric," and then handed it back to Alan.

Roarke addressed Alan and Brette then. "I know I have no real authority to command you two young men, but I will try, anyway."

The two boys nodded at the older man and listened.

"If I die tomorrow, get on your horses and ride as hard as you can back to Castle Thraill, and deliver those messages to my family."

Brette said, "We will, my Lord."

Alan was about to protest, but Roarke stopped him. "I have no idea how many men and boys have responded to King Ruric's plea for a champion—"

"Probably over a hundred," interjected Keltur.

67

Roarke nodded. "—and now they are all dead. It is in my heart to spare the two of you."

"My Lord—" Alan said.

Roarke's voice rose slightly. "I am Cedric Roarke, Lord of Thraill and Lord of Blythecairne. I have been knighted by King Ruric, and twice commissioned by Queen Maygret. I am the Dragon-Killer. Alan!" he said, his tone growing less severe, "if you absolutely must do battle with this dragon, there will still be time after you deliver my messages. God knows these things. If I die tomorrow … take my messages to my family."

Alan looked at him, not certain whether to be frustrated or grateful. "I … will do as you have requested."

Roarke nodded at him, not smiling. "I am so tired, my friends. One way or another, my journey ends tomorrow. But now, I must sleep."

"You sleep now, Sir Roarke," Keltur agreed. "And we will blanket you with our prayers tonight."

Roarke nodded. "Thank you." He lay down and covered himself with a cloak, and was asleep almost immediately.

Chapter Thirteen

"Piper said that Lord Roarke's gone off to fight the dragon!" Will said, bursting into Esselte Smead's study.

"True," Smead said sadly.

King of the Dragon scurried along behind Will, fearful of being left behind.

"Please be seated, the both of you," Smead directed.

Will felt like more than that was required—some kind of action—but not knowing what, he compliantly perched on the edge of the seat that Smead indicated.

"I should go after him," Will said.

"No, I don't believe so," Smead replied thoughtfully. "I don't think Lord Roarke ever intended you to be a part of this battle."

Will remembered his own prayer that God should find someone else to kill this dragon, and felt ashamed, guilty. He didn't even know when he had changed his mind, but he repeated, "I should go. He'll need me!"

Smead continued, "You know, Sir Tellis of the king's knights came seeking volunteers just before you rode to the northlands. And Lord Roarke compelled him to wait until after you left before making his plea ... I don't think he wanted you to hear it."

Will was somewhat surprised at this revelation, but he was not deterred. "Yes, but that was *before*. He got a queen's commission, or something? Before that, he didn't think he was going to fight the dragon himself! Or else he woulda took me!"

Smead looked at Will patiently, thoughtfully, and made a steeple with his fingers in front of his mouth. He said slowly, "Do you know who Roarke loves even more than he loves you?"

Will stared at Smead for a long moment before answering, then bit out, "Who?"

"His niece, Piper. And the two of you together, why, he loves you both so much as to just about burst his heart. I've known Cedric Roarke for many long years, and I know this to be true. Sir Willum," he continued, "no one is denying your valor. But I believe in my heart that Lord Roarke desired for you to stay here and, well … for you to stay with Piper." He smiled a tired, cheerless smile. "Someone wise and bold will have to lead these people when Roarke is too old … he has chosen you, I am sure."

"Well, he never told me that," Will said sullenly.

"I am certain that if he returns from this last battle, he will tell you all that is in his heart. But for now, isn't it clear that he did not want to expose you to this danger? Elsewise, he would have waited for your return."

Will's forehead furrowed with frustration, and he fought for words to continue his argument. "It's just … wrong," he said.

Smead agreed, "It is surely regrettable. But maybe, at last, this makes an end of it."

Will paused, lost in his own thoughts.

"What if it don't?" asked King of the Dragon, who had sat quietly listening up until now.

"Then…." Smead was at a loss for that answer. "Then…." He gave up.

"I'll go," King of the Dragon said.

Will and Smead looked at him incredulously. Will wanted to dissuade him, but was reluctant to say something that might injure his tender feelings.

The little kobold continued, "I got magic, ye know. I kilt one o' them bastids afore. I'll jist need some'un t' show me how t' get there."

Smead had heard the story of the Cave of Mendor. He said, "You are a brave and worthy fellow, O King. If Lord Roarke cannot defeat the dragon, then it may be that we will all have to contribute in whatever way that we can. It is good to know that, if you are called upon, you are willing."

"Thankee," the King said humbly.

"So ... what *should* I do, then?" Will said with unenthusiastic resignation.

Smead offered a paternal smile. "Live here. Live here at Castle Thraill until we receive word from Lord Roarke. Be who you are. Visit with our troops. Court Piper. Make your friend here comfortable in his new home. And I suppose that Cedric would ask you to pray, too."

Smead hoped that the matter had been settled and seemed to be about to dismiss the pair, but then he said, "I am worried for my old friend, too. Of course I am. But ... he has done this before. I expect he will prevail."

"I sure hope," Will said.

"As do I.... May it be so."

Chapter Fourteen

Roarke woke with the dawn, feeling refreshed, and was glad of it. He lay serenely on the rigid ground watching the eastern sky gradually brighten. He didn't sing out loud, but in his mind he prayed the words to his morning hymn:

For blessings you shall bring today,
  I thank You, God.
Whate'er adventures come my way,
  I thank You, God.
You hear me when I humbly pray,
  You keep me safe, my fears allay.
I trust Your goodness, come what may—
  I thank You, God.

He smiled up at the heavens, and realized that he was hungry. Calling softly to Brette, he woke him and asked, "Could I prevail upon you to make me some breakfast while I pray?"

"Certainly, my Lord." Brette crawled out from under his covers, eager to serve, and began building a fire.

Roarke threw off his cloak as well and walked away from the camp in order to relieve his bladder. The ground was covered with a light glittering frost, and a misty vapor rose into the air, gracing the plain with a spectral beauty. Roarke imagined for a moment that the mists were the spirits of those who had surrendered their lives in Solemon, rising regretfully to the heavens, and it sobered him somewhat.

"Well, Almighty God ... here I am, Your servant. I guess I don't have too much to say." He walked a little way further from the camp; Keltur and Alan and Porcatie were beginning to stir. "You know my heart. You know my desires. You know I want to live. You know I want to go home to the wife you gave me, to my little boy, my little gift from God."

Keltur stood and watched Roarke walking, unsure whether to join him.

Roarke continued praying, "I don't mean to sound as if I'm the only man on earth ... the only one You care about. I grieve for all of the men who have already died, whose arms also ached for their wives and their children, who will never more be filled. And I am angry ... angry at a being so foul, so evil, that it would kill for no other reason than ... that it loves to kill.

"You showed me something of what that creature was like, when You showed me what it did to Boof, what it did to Herm. Until then, I was prepared to believe that the serpent was just a reptile, just an insensate animal. But I know now, it's something worse ... it's something that *hates*. Hates men ... hates God.

"My prayer is that You would rid Hagenspan of this terrible evil ... and I also pray that You would use me to do it. Because I am here now, and if You use me ... then no one else has to die."

Alan Poppleton came softly up beside Roarke, and said, "Pardon me, my Lord, but Brette says the breakfast is ready."

"That's fine," Roarke said, and walked with him back to the camp.

ɼ

Breakfast was mostly silent. Keltur made a couple of abortive attempts at conversation, but there was little help from the others, and it was quickly abandoned.

Roarke wished wryly that the breakfast had been delicious, that it had been memorable, that the exchange of dialogue had been sparkling and inspiring. But it was not. The food was just food, suitable for providing energy for the day, but bland and tasteless otherwise. And the camaraderie consisted of five mainly glum and taciturn men sitting in a circle staring at the fire.

Realizing that it was pointless to prolong the waiting, Roarke thanked Brette for the food, asked the men to remember him in prayer, stood, and walked over to Justice. The other four men rose to their feet as well, and waited a respectful distance away.

"In case I don't come back ... thank you for your wonderful service to me," Roarke told his horse. "It's been a pleasure knowing you."

Turning back to his companions, he asked Alan, "Got my letters?" Alan nodded soberly. "Then, goodbye, my friends. May God grant that we meet again at the end of this day." He grasped their hands, turned toward the east, took a deep breath, checked his sword, and began walking toward Solemon.

ך

Roarke strode briskly toward his destiny, marching at a quick, steady pace. He had intended to pray some more as he walked, but he soon found that the evenly measured rhythm of his stride was conducive to making his mind wander ... into music. And, to his amusement, he found that the song the minstrels had composed for Hollie made a perfect marching song. He absent-mindedly hummed such parts of it as he could remember, breathing the words softly as he tramped toward Solemon.

As he sang, another part of him was indeed praying silently, an almost mindless chant.

God, bless my family ... with a hey-nonny-nonny, hey nonny-oh ... Keep them safe and strong and healthy, even if I never make it home ... hey-nonny-nonny, hey nonny-oh ... God, let me win this day ... let me kill this serpent and drive this curse from the earth ... Hey-Hollie-Hollie, hey nonny-nonny, hey Hollie-Hollie, hey nonny-oh!

He then tried praying aloud to see if that would still his distractions, and found that it helped somewhat. "There were things that I wished to do yet ... I had hoped to see Your words published throughout all Hagenspan, and the knowledge of Your ways increased. I had hoped ... that I could help....

"And I wished for things for myself, too, of course ... I don't mean to sound like I'm being completely selfless. But You knew that, too, as You know all things, I expect.

"I don't intend to represent myself as more noble than I am, for You *know* who I am. Nor do I say that I am less than I am ... for that too would be attempting to lie to God, and I doubt that You would be pleased with that any more than the other. I am just here, here for Your purposes, just me, who You know me to be."

By this time Roarke was drawing quite near the southern reaches of Solemon, where the king's crossbows lay, one unfired, one in ruins. He had half expected to meet the dragon here, before he actually reached the village, and walked with his sword drawn. He glanced at the weapons, momentarily impressed by the ingenuity of their design. Then he gently chastised himself for succumbing to yet another distraction.

"Here I am, God Almighty. I offer myself to You now. Let me be Your right arm, and rid the earth of this menace. But … if, in Your wisdom, You have some other plan … then may Your will be done." He nodded to himself, approving. "May Your will be done … let the will of God be accomplished today."

Chapter Fifteen

Creighton whispered to Sir Tellis, "Those sound like footsteps ... a man's footsteps, I mean."

Tellis put a finger to his lips, urging silence.

Paddy Clay said, softly but angrily, "What's the matter with you boys? If it's a man, it ain't the dragon!" He clambered to his feet and crept to the shattered storefront of Bedford's Tap. The four surviving Defenders of Solemon had found that the back room of this building still offered shelter that was as decent as any in Solemon, and they figured that since the dragon had already ravaged this building once, it was less likely to suspect that that was their hiding place now.

Roarke walked into the town square of Solemon, and saw the same kind of devastation he had known in his other three experiences with dragons. Everything that could be smashed was smashed; every growing thing that could be uprooted was uprooted. He wondered again what kind of malevolence it was that desired nothing but destruction and death—what was in it for the dragon? What benefit— what profit? Just to spit in the face of God?

Then he saw a man gesturing to him from the front of a smashed storefront, and he smiled grimly and walked to him. Sheathing his sword, he reached for the other's hand and said, "I know you, don't I?"

"Aye, Lord Roarke. I visited you at Blythecairne quite awhile back, and told you that this dragon—"

"Of course, I remember. How good it is to find you alive! Are there more of you?"

"Only three. All lads from Ruric's Keep—Tellis and Creighton and Hauer."

"Where are they?"

"Back inside, there. They've, ah … they've lost heart."

Roarke gave Paddy a look of commiseration and clapped him softly on the shoulder. "Where's the dragon?"

"I don't know. It leaves sometimes. It'll be back."

And then Roarke saw it. "Get inside," he hissed. Paddy obeyed immediately, and Roarke turned to face the serpent.

ſ

The dragon rose regally in the midmorning sunshine, glistening green and gold and orange, the largest of the four dragons Roarke had seen. Its breath rose from its nostrils in little puffs of vapor, and it *did* look like smoke. An irrational fear that this dragon really could spout fire clutched Roarke's chest momentarily, but he forced himself to breathe, and stepped forward into the square.

The demons in the serpent recognized him.

Instead of charging the little knight with feet thundering and teeth bared, the dragon halted where it was, its tail twitching, and bellowed a greeting.

"ROOOAAAAAARRRRRRRRRRKE!"

Roarke was amazed. He had listened tolerantly to the reports that this dragon had learned some facility of speech, but had discounted the stories as hysteria. But now ... he could not deny that it really sounded as if the beast were saying his name.

He drew his sword and took one cautious step closer.

The dragon repeated its deafening greeting.

"Are you Herm?" Roarke asked uncertainly, wondering if he should even speak to the foul beast. Perhaps fear was causing him to lose his grasp on his sanity.

The dragon nodded its head up and down, up and down, snarling. Then it said, "MMMMOOOOOOOAAAAAAAAARRRRRRRR!"

"More?" Roarke asked.

"WEEEARRRRRAAWWWWIIHHHHEEEEEEEEAAAAAAARR-RRRR!" the dragon grumbled, its mouth contorting in a yowling effort to speak human words.

"I'm sorry," Roarke said, perplexed, "but I don't understand you."

The dragon thumped its tail sharply down on the ground, causing the square to shake. It bellowed furiously then, and Roarke was fairly certain that it wasn't trying to say anything, but still the dragon did not charge. Roarke noticed that the uppermost parts of the dragon's shoulders were trembling, almost as if it were trying to break free from some kind of invisible bonds, but its feet stayed rooted to the ground.

"I feel fairly certain that we are not destined to become friends," Roarke said, "and however impressive it is that you have taught this beast to mumble a few barely coherent words, you are still a vile murderer, a foul fiend, and the Almighty will truly have His vengeance upon you, be it today or someday still aways off."

The dragon growled a low warning. "I curse you for the lives of the good men of Hagenspan that you have wasted." His voice began to rise. "I curse you for Beale's Keep! I curse you for Lauren and Blythecairne!" The dragon lifted a foot. "I curse you for Solemon! In the name of the Lord Iesuchristi the Almighty God, I curse you!" At the speaking of that name, the serpent tipped its head back and keened, as if the name itself portended the beast's mortality.

Roarke saw that the dragon was livid with frustrated rage, and murmured, "Let us begin this dance." He stepped toward his foe.

Chapter Sixteen

Piper was waiting in the stables when Will walked in. "I thought you might come here," she said dejectedly.

"I thought I might take Starlight out for a little ride," he said, feeling a bit sheepish.

"And were you planning on returning?"

"Of course," he said. His cheeks felt hot.

"Then help me saddle Buttercup, and I'll ride with you."

"All right."

꙳

Roarke stalked warily around in a circle, facing the serpent, which did likewise. He held his sword in his right hand, his arm relaxed but ready. He stepped cautiously over ruts that the dragon had gouged in the street, making slow circles with the tip of his blade.

The serpent crept closer, growling its low rumbling pique.

Suddenly, the beast whipped its reptilian tail toward the knight, but it was not close enough to strike him. Roarke took a step backwards, stepped in a rut and almost lost his footing, but quickly recovered. Then the dragon stabbed at him with its snout, and Roarke's blade flashed upward, dealing the beast a stinging slice on the end of its blunt nose.

The dragon jerked its head backward in surprise, and a trickle of blood appeared.

ʔ

King of the Dragon liked Esselte Smead, who seemed to know more about kobolds than even Tilda and Vesta had. He certainly knew more about what they liked to drink.

"What d'ye call this stuff again?" he asked.

Smead said, "We call it 'mead.' We make it right here at the castle." In fact, the brew that King of the Dragon was drinking had been mixed with water to make it a little less potent for the little gray fellow, who was unaccustomed to fermented drinks.

"Mead," King of the Dragon chortled happily. "Mead. Smead. Mead. Smead."

The steward of Thraill smiled, offered a good-natured chuckle.

"Did I tell ye aboot when I kilt th' dragon?"

"I'd be happy to hear it again," Smead said.

ʔ

Roarke continued to circle warily around the dragon as it lifted its face to the cold morning sky and raged. This was a dangerous time—the beast was angry, but had not lost anything like enough blood to be weakened at all. It whipped its tail back and forth violently, sending stones and debris skittering across the square in every direction.

Bending its massive head down to roar furiously at the white-haired knight, the dragon received another slash across its snout, and red blood spurted out. This enraged the beast yet more, and it stomped its wrath around the square, its muscular tail nearly swiping Roarke from his feet. He only avoided that blow by diving to the ground at the last moment, losing his grasp on his blade in the process. But he clambered back to his feet and grabbed the sword again before the dragon could realize that he had been momentarily weaponless.

The dragon stopped and tipped its head back, howling, and Roarke seized the chance to rush forward and thrust the point of his blade toward the beast's lessprotected underbelly. He didn't strike a solid blow, but did prick the dragon between a couple of scales, causing another trickle of blood to seep down its torso.

ſ

Padallor Clay heard the outraged roaring of the dragon. It was a different sound than that which it usually made—there was a hint of pain in the cry. "Tellis! Let's watch! It's Roarke, and the dragon ain't just killed him, like it did everyone else!"

Hauer jostled Creighton, and said, "Let's see."

The four Defenders of Solemon, more hopeful than they had been for as long as they could recall, crept to the shadows just inside the window of Bedford's Tap, arriving just in time to see Roarke make a second thrust with his sword toward the dragon's midsection. The white-haired knight scored a piercing, agonizing hit upon the serpent's stomach, and the blood streamed from the beast's wounds, beginning to spatter upon the dirt of the square.

"What a remarkable man," Paddy breathed, filled with awe and pride.

ɼ

Roarke was clearly winning the battle, but he was starting to pant, and his right arm was growing weary from the weight of his sword. Also, his ankle was starting to throb where he had turned it earlier, when he had stepped awkwardly in the rutted street.

He stumbled a little as he circled the dragon, but the beast was so consumed with its own anguish that it did not notice.

The dragon licked its snout where the blood was beginning to dribble into its mouth. It tossed its head to the left, to the right, trying to rid itself of the sharp pain on the tip of its stunted nose. It snapped its tail toward its bitter enemy, but again missed the knight.

ɼ

Haldamar Tenet looked up from his desk and saw his wife coming into the room. "Where've you been?" he asked. "I was looking for you earlier."

Ronica looked away from him, and he could tell that she had been crying. "I've just been ... taking a walk in the garden ... saying a prayer for my brother." She rubbed her wrist, and Haldamar could see that she was in pain.

"What have you done?"

"I'm ashamed to say."

He pushed his chair back, stood, and took her in his arms. "You don't need to be."

She rested her head against his shoulder. After a moment, she said, "I took a sword from the armory and went out to the garden ... and struck ... the stone dragon." Her upper lip began to tremble. "It bounced right off."

ʃ

Roarke continued to circle cautiously, warily, wearily, around the wounded dragon. He tried to force himself to breathe through his nose, but wasn't getting enough air that way, so he opened his mouth and drew in ragged gasps of air.

A salty drop of sweat rolled down from his forehead into the corner of his left eye, stinging. He tried to blink it away, but that only succeeded in blurring his vision. He pressed his left eye tightly shut, wincing, squinting through his right eye, trying to keep the dragon in focus.

The dragon's tail struck him from his blind side, knocking him from his feet. He bounced and skidded across the rutted ground, and his sword went flying off several paces away from where he landed. Roarke was aware of a brief sensation of pain, and then the world turned dark.

Ruric the King perched nervously upon his throne, adjudicating over the trifling matters of the kingdom, the affairs of people who little understood the sacrifice that was being made in Solemon. Finally he said, "Enough for today! I can bear no more of this!"

Sometime later his queen came to him with concern evident upon her features. "I have heard that you dismissed your court. Are you well?"

"I will hardly rest until I have heard from Jayles," the old man complained. "Or, for that matter, from Keltur. Why hasn't he returned with news of Roarke?"

Maygret patted his hand gently. "Still your fears, my King. I believe that when this battle is won, the people will not be singing the praises of Roarke, or of Jayles either. I believe your ingenious weapon will provide this victory, and the people of Hagenspan will shout for Serpent's-Bane. They will shout at last for Serpent's-Bane." She smiled at him and looked into his eyes.

He smiled back, feebly, gratefully.

The dragon limped over to where Roarke lay on the ground, his body twisted at a grotesque angle. The beast appeared to be confused, disoriented. It seemed to be … disappointed.

It bent down low over the knight's twisted body, and called, "ROOO-OOAAAAAAARRRRRKE!"

A drop of blood from the dragon's nose spattered down upon the fallen knight, and the beast bent lower to sniff the body. The serpent nudged the man with the end of its snout, but still he did not stir. Again the dragon pled, "RRROOOOOOOOOOOAAAAAAAAAAAAARRRRRRRKE!"

꜀

Hollie's heart was grieved, distressed by the want of her husband ... but still she had to go on. If not for herself, then for Owan. Her own baby boy.

Owan was too young to recognize the absence of his father, but Hollie was sure that the little boy recognized, somehow, the sadness of his mother.

So she smiled and spoke softly to him as he nursed, and he stared back into her eyes, unblinking, until sleep began to beckon, and his own eyelids grew too heavy for him to hold open any longer.

She sang to her boy, in a barely audible voice, the lullaby she had learned from Jesi Tenet, until his neck relaxed, his head sagged backward, and his tiny mouth released its suckling kiss from her breast.

> *Sleep, little baby, sleep—*
> *safe in the arms that love you.*
> *Dream, little baby, dream—*
> *nothing can harm you now.*

꜀

The dragon straightened up and scanned the battlefield, sending a meaningful glare toward Bedford's Tap. It grumbled its discontent, a low throbbing pulsation of anger. Suddenly the blood-spattered beast was very, very tired.

Bending its head down to the unmoving man one last time, it complained, "ROOOAAAARRRRKE!"

When the man did not respond, the dragon raised its massive leg and prepared to crush whatever remained of life out of Roarke's broken body.

Chapter Seventeen

Roarke was stunned—dazed by the blow from the dragon's cordlike tail, and knocked temporarily senseless when his head struck the ground. The side of his face was scraped and bleeding, and his left arm was bent at an awkward angle away from his body, useless.

But the dragon's final earsplitting plaint had been enough to stir him, to draw him groggily back toward consciousness. He woke, trying to remember where he was, rolled stiffly over onto his back with a little gasp of pain, and saw the claws of the reptilian foot poised over his head, just beginning to descend.

Suddenly he was with his father, and it was the first time he had ever been allowed to leave the family farm, going with his father to market in Lauren. A mixture of surprise and delight washed over him, and he said, "Daddy, I'm so happy to see you!" And his father looked pleased and a little confused, and said, "I've always been right here, Cedric."

And then Millisen filled his eyes, good Millisen, plain but attractive at the same time, and he recalled how much he had loved her as a youth, and how amazed he had been that she had chosen him. He remembered how shy and clumsy they had been the first time they had made love, and how happy and proud they had felt when they were through. He saw her smiling from the front door of their little farmhouse, and he raised his hand to greet her, but she was gone.

Then another face filled his vision, and to Roarke's sorrow, her features appeared to him more clearly than had Millisen's. She was fair-haired, she was laughing, bringing him beer, pressing herself against him. He remembered the sound of her laughter. He remembered what she

91

smelled like. Her name was Alissa, and she was the barmaid from Lauren. How curious that he should recall her name now, Roarke thought.

Before he had a chance to apologize to her for his conduct, Roarke saw his farm, destroyed, destroyed by the dragon. And once again, the agony flowed into his belly, the bereavement, the bitter torment. He wanted to retch, he wanted to weep.

And then a succession of serpents—one, two, three—falling before his blade. And he felt no joy in those victories, only guilt and remorse for the blackness of his sin.

While he was still experiencing the emptiness of his own soul, he remembered his visit from Barnabas, and the three scraps of God's words that he still wore around his neck, the words that had restored hope to his life, that had given him a renewed sense of purpose. He felt for the pouch now, and found it where it belonged, and felt a pang of regret that he had not left it with Alan Poppleton to take home to Owan—maybe it would have been meaningful to him someday.

He remembered Owan … and the incredible joy he had felt when he had known that God had counted some little part of himself as worthy to endure—worthy to pass on to another generation. He wished to say one last quick prayer for Owan, but there wasn't time. There wasn't time.

And then his vision dissolved into a golden swirl, and the swirl became a tangle of golden hair, and the hair framed the loveliest face he had ever seen in the long years of his sojourn. He saw Hollie, laughing as she had laughed when he had first seen her from across Kenndt's dining room. He saw her angry and full of fire during the tumultuous days of their courtship. And he saw her beautiful face contort with pain, and begin spilling tears, tears that became a river of sorrow, that filled the Great Sea, that filled the world, that filled the sky. "It's all right, Hollie," he tried to say. "It doesn't hurt anymore."

And her face faded, and became light—light, a glowing orb, like the sun, like the sun shining full bright, but it did not hurt his eyes. And he began to rise toward the light, and his heart grew exceedingly glad.

And the dragon's foot fell.

Chapter Eighteen

Hauer and Creighton saw the dragon step on Roarke's body and grind him into the ground, and they both fled for the back room, heartsick and afraid. Paddy and Tellis also saw, and stood rooted where they were, horrified.

"My God ... what could it mean?" Paddy exclaimed.

"He's dead. Roarke's dead," Tellis said with dark dismay.

"He can't be," Paddy gasped.

"He's dead," Tellis repeated. "Come on." He grabbed Paddy by the shirtsleeve and tugged him back toward the room in the rear of Bedford's Tap, where the other two were cowering, weeping.

"I don't understand," Paddy said, and looked back over his shoulder toward the bloody street.

"It's the end of all things," Sir Tellis said grimly.

"What?" said Hauer, with a wild look in his eyes.

Tellis said, "For Hagenspan, anyway ... it's the end of all things."

"Why?" Creighton asked.

"The best men in Hagenspan have come to Solemon and they have all died. Now, maybe the very best man of us all is dead with them. There will be nothing to stop this dragon. Nothing. It will have us all." The coolness of Tellis' voice made it sound as if he were simply exercising logic, but his eyes were feral and his brow was beaded with a feverish perspiration.

The other three Defenders of Solemon paused to assess the truthfulness of Tellis' assertion, and it seemed to them that it easily might be as he had said.

"Maybe ... Roarke ain't dead," Paddy wished.

"He's dead. Stop that talk," Tellis commanded.

"I know. It's just ... hard."

"It's hard for all of us." Tellis changed the subject. "What are we going to do now?"

"*Do?*" Hauer said incredulously, and Creighton began to laugh quietly, a little deranged.

Tellis, a little of his old self-respect returning, snapped, "What do *you* want to do? Stay here hiding in this hole until we starve to death?" Angry flecks of spittle flew from his lips. "Wouldn't you rather go out and finish spending your life by trying to kill this abomination against everything that is holy?"

Hauer's voice began to rise as well. "You want to just go out and sacrifice yourself to the dragon, do it!"

"Quietly, boys," Paddy Clay warned. "It's still out there, you know."

"What difference does that make?" Hauer demanded.

"I don't know," Paddy admitted. "But let's stop and think for a bit."

Creighton started softly crying again, and said, "It's killed everybody that's gone up against it—must be dozens, or *dozens* of dozens. What good can we do? We're just four men!"

Paddy frowned for a moment, but then had an idea and brightened. "We're not just four men…. We're four men with one whoppin' big bow and arrow."

They looked at each other and waited to see if perhaps something like hope might start to grow within their breasts. Hauer said tentatively, "The dragon's probably smashed it."

"Well, let's see, before we give up," Paddy urged.

"Are *you* going to go?" Creighton said, with an offended tone in his voice.

"Hell, yes. The dragon's hurt. If Roarke had had a few more minutes, he mighta killed it. We'll never have a better chance than now."

"That's right," Tellis said; he had not thought of that.

"You'll go with me?" Paddy asked Tellis, and the knight nodded bleakly, but with determination.

"How does it work? The bow, I mean." Paddy asked Creighton and Hauer.

Creighton began to answer, "There's this big handle—" but Hauer interrupted him with, "We'll go with you."

Creighton's face was striped with furrows that his tears had made through the grime. He had a wounded look in his eyes, but did not protest.

Hauer looked at him hard and said, "What's it matter? Die quick out there—die slow in here. Might as well go out as heroes if we have the choice. Even if it is suicide."

Creighton shook his head forlornly, but the men could tell that he was not disagreeing with them.

Paddy asked, meaning the dragon, "Is it still out front?"

"Wait. I'll look," Sir Tellis said.

A moment later, he was back, saying, "It seems to be sleeping in the square next to Roarke. Next to his body."

"Well, maybe it'll just die right there, if Roarke got it good enough." He breathed a silent prayer that it would be so. "But at least we know where it is for a change. Let's slip out the back and run real quiet down to where that bow is."

"Shouldn't we sleep a mite first?" asked Creighton, who was indeed feeling very much exhausted.

"One way or the other, there'll be plenty of time for sleepin' tomorrow."

Chapter Nineteen

From the southwest of Solemon, Alan, Brette, Porcatie, and Sir Keltur could faintly hear the outraged roaring of the dragon throughout the late morning, and they knew the battle had commenced. Then, about midday, the roaring ceased.

All through the afternoon, the four men waited with nervous expectation, hoping to see Roarke walking toward them from the village, announcing that the dragon was dead. He did not come.

As evening began to cast its long shadows across the frozen countryside, an icy wind began to blow down from the mountains and across the plain. The men, who had debated sporadically through the afternoon about what they should do, sunk into a sullen silence, wrapping themselves closely in their cloaks.

After another fretful hour had passed, Porcatie gloomily said to Brette and Alan, "Maybe you boys ought to get a little start back toward Castle Thraill before it gets full dark."

Brette started to nod, but Alan protested. "We don't know that Lord Roarke is dead! We don't know anything of the kind! The dragon stopped roaring, and it may be that Roarke killed it."

"He hasn't returned," Porcatie reasoned.

"No, but he may be injured," Sir Keltur interjected. "As much as I would like to see Alan and Brette headed off toward safety, we must know. We can't send the boys off to tell Lady Hollie that her husband's dead without being certain."

"But...." Porcatie didn't complete the thought.

"I'll go," Keltur said. "Wait here until you hear from me. If I don't return by morning, ride like the wind for Castle Thraill."

"What should I do?" Porcatie asked.

"If I don't return, then Roarke is dead. Ride his horse and deliver it back to his widow."

"Sir Keltur … maybe I should come with you," Porcatie ventured.

"Thank you, but no. If the dragon is not dead, then I am better served by stealth than strength." He prepared to mount up. "I will tether my horse to the broken crossbow and go the rest of the way on foot. Remember—if I am not back by morning, don't wait for me."

ſ

Sir Tellis led the Defenders of Solemon through what remained of the village, amazed at how completely the dragon had ruined every seemingly insignificant part of the community. There was no house left in the village that would ever be lived in again without first undergoing considerable repair; there were only scant patches of vegetation that had not been deracinated.

They crept through the back yards of Solemon, sneaking from uprooted tree to pile of debris to broken wall, avoiding any place that was visible from the street, even though they knew they had left the wounded dragon languidly dozing in the square. Paddy followed Tellis, Creighton came next, and Hauer brought up the rear.

They reached a pile of boards and rubble that represented the southernmost house of Solemon, and peered out across the field toward the locations at both sides of the King's Road where the crossbows were stationed, one of them still loaded and pointing more or less toward their own hiding place.

The four men crouched behind the wreckage and uneasily scanned their surroundings, gathering the courage to step out from their place of concealment and head across the open ground to the weapons. As Tellis was about to move out, though, Paddy grabbed his arm and pointed in the direction of the crossbows.

"What?" Tellis demanded in a harsh whisper.

Paddy looked at him, and pointed again.

Bobbing up over the crest of a knoll came the head of a man, then his shoulders, then the head of the horse he was astride. The fading sunlight was behind him, so he appeared only as a black form against the grayness of the plain, but Tellis whispered, "It must be a knight."

"Should we warn him?" Paddy asked.

"About what?" Tellis replied. "There are no knights who don't know about Solemon."

"Oh ... of course."

Tellis made a decision and said, "You three wait here. I am going to the knight."

ſ

The dragon wanted to sleep now … to sleep. The little knight was dead, the one that she knew she hated for some reason, hated more than all the other humans combined.

Her head rested on the ground, next to the body of her adversary. She stared at him coolly through one narrow slit of an eye. The wind blowing through the square rustled the man's white hair, but other than that, there was no movement. She thought distractedly that perhaps she would eat him, but strangely felt rather ambivalent about the idea. She wanted to sleep.

The voices inside her were nearly silent now—apparently they had been satisfied. Nearly.

But then other pictures began to play in her mind, memories of other times and other places—places where she was not certain she even been before. She saw a narrow stairwell that she could not ascend, and beyond her reach was a morsel that almost drove her mad not to be able to taste. And there was a scent, too, a cloying, sickening smell like the purple-flowered trees that she hated so much. The stomach-turning odor trailed up the stairwell, the place she could not reach, no matter how she tried to wedge her head into it. And then the scent seemed to drift off, across the miles and across the years, and she was in the body of a human, sitting across a table from the one who wore the scent. And again, she could not bite, she could not tear, even though she wanted to ravage the golden-haired woman who emitted the galling stench, and rip her limb from limb.

She sensed a voice, a small voice inside her trying to incite the other voices, and even though the others seemed indifferent, they agreed at last with the one small voice, and together they began to grow more insistent again, to enflame the serpent to anger, to become an unyielding compulsion within her, bending her will to theirs. They would not let her sleep.

Lurching laboriously to her feet, she bellowed her frustrated rage.

Chapter Twenty

Keltur galloped back to the camp where he had left Alan, Brette, and Porcatie. They stood there waiting anxiously for his news.

"Mount up!" he ordered. "Ride tonight. Go slowly in the dark so you don't injure your horses, but go as far west as you can go tonight."

Alan knew what this command meant, but Brette asked anyway, his brow furrowed with concern. "Lord Roarke?"

Keltur said grimly, "There are a few men left in Solemon, a few who still stand against the dragon, including Sir Tellis. They are getting ready to make their last defense, and I will be joining them. They, ah, saw Sir Roarke fall. He is dead," he added, in case there was any doubt.

Porcatie, who had seen what the dragon was capable of, felt somewhat lightheaded, but blinked, swallowed, and said, "I will stay with you, Sir Keltur."

"I thought you might. You are welcome, of course."

Brette said, "Lord Roarke's horse."

"Yes?" Keltur asked.

"It should be delivered back to Castle Thraill. Forgive me ... but I would ride Lord Roarke's horse, and Porcatie may take mine. If you think...?" This was actually a significant sacrifice on Brette's part, for he was very fond of his own horse.

Keltur nodded, and said, "Well thought of, young man. Make it so."

A few minutes more of preparation, and then the four men were shaking hands and making solemn farewells. Then Alan and Brette began heading west toward the sunset, and Keltur and Porcatie turned back toward Solemon.

ʃ

Tellis breathlessly reported to the Defenders of Solemon, "It's Sir Keltur— we are most fortunate! He has three men with him, but he is sending them back to Thraill with news of Roarke. After that, though, he is returning to us to lead us in the fight." Tellis looked at his comrades hopefully. "We will not have a better chance to defeat the dragon. It's been wounded, it must be tired from the fight with Roarke, and now we have Keltur."

"Keltur's a good one?" Paddy asked.

"Sir Keltur is the captain of the king's guard," Tellis said shortly.

"Well, that ain't just a ceremonial position, is it?"

"No. Keltur is a true man." Tellis' eyes blazed in defense of his friend.

"Welcome, then," Paddy said. "Just askin'."

Tellis continued, "Sir Keltur is also the one who summoned Sir Roarke from the west, and he rode here across Hagenspan with him. He is probably the most qualified man in the whole country to lead this defense."

Hauer and Creighton knew Keltur, and they did not need to be convinced.

"Let's go," Hauer said. "We're wasting what's left of the light."

Paddy said, "That's right. Sorry, lads. Why don't you three go and get ready to work the weapon, and I'll see if I can lure the beastie in."

"No," said Tellis. "We'll all go to the bow, and wait for Sir Keltur. Then he can decide what our best course of action is."

"As you say," Paddy said agreeably. He had been aware of the possibility of his own death for several weeks, and it didn't much matter to him whether he was in front of the crossbow or behind it. He had survived in Solemon longer than any of the other defenders, and he wished to see the dragon dead if he could, but he wasn't so conceited that he thought his plan would necessarily be better than that of the knights.

The men stepped cautiously out from their hiding place amid the wreckage, and began creeping across the field toward the undamaged weapon. They were halfway there when the dragon came staggering from the end of town, its belly covered with a slick coating of blood, but still deadly, still furious.

Keltur and Porcatie, who were too far away to help, saw the huge reptile stalking the four dark figures, and shouted and waved, but their cries went unnoticed. They saw from a distance as the serpent caught up with the men, seizing one of them in its jaws and pitching him high into the air.

That unhappy man was Creighton, and he was quickly joined in his journey to the next world by Sir Tellis, who was likewise caught up and flung head over heels into the graying dusk.

Paddy shouted to Hauer, "Run to the bow! I'll try to distract it!"

Hauer sprinted the rest of the way across the open ground to the firing mechanism of the crossbow, as the dragon caught the descending Sir Tellis with a snapping sound. Paddy Clay jumped up and down, waving his arms and shouting incoherently, trying to make the dragon turn away from following Hauer.

Far across the plain, Keltur knew that the moment of his testing had arrived, and cried to Porcatie, "Ride!" but Porcatie drew back on his reins. Keltur was many yards across the field before he realized that the other man was no longer with him. Wheeling around and charging back to where Porcatie waited, Keltur demanded, "Are you all right?"

Porcatie, helplessly, desperately, shamed, said, "I can't."

The knight saw defeat written on Porcatie's ashen face, paused only a moment, and said, "Go!" He dug his heels into his horse's ribs, spurring him on back toward Solemon and the battle.

The dragon heard Paddy's voice, recognizing it, and bent down toward him, intent on snuffing out the annoying squeak of his cries. Paddy saw his doom approaching swiftly, and dove to the ground, rolling back up onto his feet and running, leading the pursuing serpent directly in front of the king's crossbow.

Hauer gave a huge tug on the lever and released the metal-tipped arrow with a loud *thwang*! Unprepared for the machine's violent recoil, he was thrown from the firing platform, and landed on his back on the earth with a breath-banishing thump.

The shaft hit the dragon in the left shoulder, knocking the beast to the ground with a tremendous scuffling thud, and for a few giddy seconds Paddy thought that they had won. But then the reptile scrambled back to its feet, and though it was bleeding from that shoulder, Paddy could see that the blow had been a glancing one. It may have broken the dragon's shoulder, but it had not broken the dragon.

The beast was, if possible, angrier than Paddy had yet seen it, and in its throbbing rage it turned back toward where the attack had come from, where Hauer was trying groggily to sit up. The dragon, any hint of playfulness gone, did not flip this man into the air, but viciously bit right through his torso, so that his legs and hindquarters were left sitting where they had been, but the upper part of his body was gone.

Paddy, weaponless, alone, aghast, saw only one thing left for him to do. He turned and began running as hard as he could back to Solemon, taking the shortest possible route that would lead him back to the relative safety of Bedford's Tap, if he were quick and lucky.

The dragon was almost blind with fury, but nonetheless saw Paddy trying to make his escape. Dizzy and disoriented from the blow to its shoulder and all the blood it had lost this day, the dragon staggered after him, lurching closer and closer to the fleeing man with each thundering step.

Chapter Twenty-One

Sir Keltur hurtled across the plain, seeing the dragon disappear back into the village, chasing the last survivor of Solemon. He didn't anticipate being able to save that last man, but he had seen the dragon temporarily knocked from its feet when it was struck by the arrow, and knew that he would never have a better opportunity to finish the job than now.

He reached the town and followed the rutted main street, between the smashed buildings and broken trees, and arrived in the square ready to fight. But the dragon was not there.

He wheeled around the square, trying to determine which one of the four streets the beast had gone down, but except for dismissing the direction that he had just come from, he could not tell.

Then he saw Roarke.

ŗ

Brette whispered, "It's getting awful dark, Alan. Do you think we've gone far enough for tonight?" He could just barely see the white puff of his breath as it rose in front of his face.

Alan had been dozing as he rode, and he was startled by his friend's voice. "I'm sorry ... what?"

"Do you think we can stop and sleep for a couple of hours?"

"Oh ... I don't know."

They had heard the dragon's bellows from behind them as they had ridden away from the battlefield, had heard until either they had gotten far enough away so that they could hear no longer, or else perhaps the dragon had just ceased its bawling. Then they had ridden on for a few more silent hours—Brette didn't know how many—silent except for the clopping and snorting of their horses.

"I'm so tired I almost don't care if the dragon kills me or not, just so I could sleep," Brette murmured.

"All right," Alan agreed. "We're probably safe enough." They reined up and dismounted. "Make sure you picket Roarke's horse so it doesn't wander off."

"I'm not *that* tired," Brette said.

In a matter of moments the two exhausted youths were asleep on the ice-hard ground, huddled fitfully in their cloaks against the cold.

༄

The dragon had stalked the two riders throughout the black hours of the moonless night. Even though she hurt everywhere, especially in her broken and bleeding left shoulder, the compulsion inside her would not allow her to voice her frustration, even though she wanted to moan and cry and snarl. The maddening voices would not allow her to rest, even though she longed to lie down on the ground and sleep, sleep for a hundred years.

She came to the two horses, which reared and screamed in terror when they sensed the malicious reptilian presence. Roarke's stallion, Justice, jerked his shallow picket from the earth and fled across the blackened landscape, but Alan's horse was unable to escape, and the dragon bit down upon it with a dispassionate squish. Eating was not the source of joy it had been a month ago, especially not with the persistent presence of her bodily pain.

The two humans heard their horses scream and jumped up. She figured she should eat one of them, but couldn't make herself care enough to do so. The voices inside her wanted her to sing to them.

She thumped the ground with her tail, trying to get their attention so they would listen. She wanted to go back to her wooden town and sleep. She opened her mouth and sang.

"AAAAAAAHHHHHHHHHHEEEEEEEEEEEEEEEEEEE. COM-MMMMMMMMMMME." She looked at the little creatures, who were scrabbling around on the ground, apparently trying to find weapons, so she angrily thumped the ground with her tail again, and again once more.

"AAAAAAAAAAAAAAHHHHHHHHEEEEEEEEEEE. COMM-MMMMMMMMMMMMME."

The dragon was worn out, fatigued. The voices inside her commanded her to eat one of the humans ... but she disobeyed. Snarling and snapping, she tried to bite the voices out of her own head, but could not reach them. She wanted to sleep. She must sleep. But not here. Turning away from the diminutive creatures that knelt before her, she limped back toward her town. She must sleep.

ʃ

Keltur knelt beside Roarke's body, tried to look, but quickly had to avert his eyes. He had seen enough so that he knew it was Roarke ... the white hair, the clothing. But if he had not already known who it was, he would not have been able to identify the body. He felt his stomach rebel, and fought to refrain from retching.

He silently prayed something, or wished to.

Taking a fleeting glance back down at the fallen knight, he said, "Well, my friend, you must not have suffered for long. There's that to be thankful for." Keltur peered warily around the darkened square, not knowing when or from where the dragon might return. "If I survive this coming day, I'll see that you get a proper burial." He looked around the square for rocks that might make suitable gravestones, and considered covering Roarke with his cloak, but then decided prudently that he would need his cloak for defense against the winter wind that night. "It may be that I will be joining you sooner than that."

He tugged the mantle tighter around his shoulders and shuddered. "I wonder where you are right now ... have you gone on someplace far away, or are you quite near, watching me kneel next to your body? Are you angry? Are you in pain? Or have all of those things ... become inconsequential?"

The only answer was the desolate cry of the wind, which seemed somehow fitting to Keltur. He lay down on the street and, after a moment, closed his eyes, trusting his horse to wake him if the need arose.

Chapter Twenty-Two

Piper struggled to control her emotions; she wanted to be a proper lady, dignified and elegant, like Aunt Hollie had been when Uncle Cedric had gone away. But pain was evident in her eyes, and Willum knew that he was the cause of it.

They stood in the garden, not touching, both of them huddled in robes of skin to shield them from the blowing snow. The cold caused two bright spots of color to appear on Piper's cheeks, and Will remembered how the blush in her cheeks had flared for him before, in happier days, in teasing, playful times.

"Sir Willum," she said softly, and he was saddened by the formality of her address, "I ... I had thought...."

He wanted to tell her how much he loved her, how much he wanted to spend every moment for the rest of his life with her alone, that he considered her to be the most precious thing in God's world. But he stayed silent. He stood, apart from her, looking helplessly into her eyes.

Piper tried again. "Do you ... wish to withdraw your offer of ...marriage to me?" A single tear broke from her eye and escaped down her lovely face, past her trembling lip, and disappeared, spent, at the delicate line of her jaw.

Oh, no! Will longed to say. *How could you ever think that I didn't want to marry you?* What he said was, "I don't know, Piper."

"I see." A cloud descended over her face, and it was as if Will could feel her receding from his very heart. "Well ... if you change your mind, will you let me know?"

113

He nodded, not knowing what else to do. He could hardly explain the distance that had grown between them since he had come back from the north country, except that he knew that it somehow related to Lord Roarke, the dragon, and Will's sense of duty, of responsibility. He had hoped that Piper would understand, and she probably did ... but Will didn't know what to do.

She looked at his kindly, confused face for a moment more, and felt exquisite compassion for this man, this boy, that she loved with all of her being.

She said softly, "Goodbye, Will."

No! Stop! Will's heart cried, but his lips did not speak. He watched her as she walked imperially back to the castle, and wondered how it was that she did not cry, when it felt as if his very soul were being wrenched in two. *Come back!* he called her silently, watching the wind whip her chestnut hair.

Piper walked back within the stone walls of the castle, feeling as if they were closing in around her, suffocating her, but she did not hurry her pace, not until she was walking up the stairs to her own room, where she threw herself sobbing upon her bed.

ſ

Brette and Alan had managed to catch Justice, and they both rode the magnificent black stallion westward to Haioland, hoping that Justice was strong enough to bear them both until they should arrive someplace where they might borrow a second horse.

Brette, who was riding behind Alan, said tentatively, "The dragon."

The boys had not talked much since their ordeal. Alan said, "What about it?"

"It seemed almost like it was talking to us."

"It *was* talking to us. Didn't you know?"

Brette, abashed, said, "Well ... what was it saying?"

"I thought you knew."

"Well, I got 'come.' But what was that 'Aaaahhhh-Eeeeeeeeee' part?"

Alan shook his head slightly and allowed himself a tight, grim smile. "It was 'Hollie.' The dragon was saying, 'Hollie, come.'"

"Oh!" Brette exclaimed. He chastised himself that he had not been able to figure that out on his own. "'Hollie, come.'" He thought for a moment. "That can't be good."

"No."

Finally the dragon was back in the town square, her courtyard, her chosen nesting place. But there was somebody else there—another little one like the one she had hated. The one she had loved. The one she had hated.

She could sense that this one intended to make trouble for her, and after all of the trouble she had experienced in the past day, she had no patience for the game. She swept him from the earth with one swing of her mighty tail, sending him crashing against one of the buildings of the square. He collapsed, sighed, and expired.

She lay down next to Roarke and slept.

Chapter Twenty-Three

Esselte Smead sat at his desk signing requisitions, invoices, authorizations for payment—the duties of the steward of Thraill. King of the Dragon sat nearby, occasionally taking a contented sip from a tankard of mead. He spent more time now with Smead than he did with Sir Willum, since Sir Willum was usually busy with something, and less inclined than Smead to let him just sit quietly with a tankard.

King of the Dragon had become a favorite among many of the people of the castle. To say that they viewed him as some exotic kind of pet would not be entirely accurate, but it would not be too far from the truth, either. He had his own room, sparsely furnished, with some rocks that had been carried in by a few of Thraill's young men, and a pair of wooden chairs for guests. He almost always remembered to wear pants when he left his room. With a warm belly filled with mead, and the companionship of his new friends, he was as happy as he had ever been.

A tentative knock at Smead's doorpost interrupted the steward's work, and the King's reverie. Smead looked up and saw a young man named Regehr, of Castle Thraill's Sun Company.

"Master Smead," he began.

"Master Regehr," Smead replied. "Aren't you on duty at the gate today?"

"Yes, sir," the youth answered uncomfortably.

"Then who's watching the gate?"

"Well, I am, sir," he stammered, "but I thought this was urgent—"

"What is it?" Smead asked, sudden apprehension gripping him like the tightness of a fist in his chest.

"It's Lord Poppleton's son, and his squire. They're at the gate."

"Why didn't you show them in?"

"Poppleton asked if you would please meet him outside first. He brings news."

"Of course. But why…?"

"Master Smead … one of the horses they have—"

"Yes?"

"It looks to be Lord Roarke's Justice."

"Oh?" he said blankly. Then he understood. "Oh, no."

King of the Dragon said, "What? What is it?"

"Oh, no," Smead repeated, and stood and walked slowly from the room.

Owan was sleeping at last, so Hollie had thought it was safe to steal down the back stairwell to the kitchen and fetch herself some tea. She shared a brief moment of conversation with her friend Helen, who paused from preparing bread for the evening meal, dusted her hands off on her apron and poured a cup of tea for both of them. Hollie didn't stay long, though, excusing herself so that she could head back up to where her little son slept, balancing her steaming cup on its saucer as she ascended the stairs.

When she arrived at the entrance to her rooms, though, she was startled by the presence of someone else already there, and voiced a short gasp of surprise. As her eyes quickly adjusted to the room's light, though, she saw that it was Smead, who turned apologetically to face her.

"Lady Hollie, please forgive me," Smead said, his round face filled with sorrow.

"Master Smead," she said apprehensively, and her hand began to shake, so that the teacup clattered audibly against the saucer and the tea sloshed over onto her hand, onto the floor. She tried to set the cup down on a nearby wooden stand, but misjudged the distance, and the cup fell to the floor, splashing its contents and spattering her robe with tea. "Oh," she said with a kind of bewildered calm. "Please excuse me, Esselte ... I'll need to ... it will stain." The room began swimming, and she felt lightheaded, not knowing whether to giggle or sob.

"Hollie," Smead said, reaching out to steady her, keep her from falling.

"No, that's all right," she said, shaking her head, but taking his hand and holding on. "I know why you're here ... it's bad news. It's bad news, isn't it?" Her eyes began to fill. "Is it ... the worst?"

Smead closed his eyes and nodded grimly.

Hollie felt that her knees had become powerless to hold her upright, and stumbled toward her chair. Smead assisted her into the seat, and she looked at him helplessly, saying, "Oh, Cedric...."

"May I get you anything, my dear? May I get somebody to stay with you?" Smead asked sadly.

119

"No ... no, I suppose not," Hollie murmured, looking around at the things in her room as if she had never seen them before. Her eyes came to rest on the caring face of Esselte Smead. "Master Smead, I am suddenly very tired. Do you think you could find someone to come and watch—" She stopped, baffled. "I'm sorry, but I've forgotten the name of that baby."

Smead was embarrassed for her, but thought he understood that she was suffering from the shock of the news he hadn't even had to tell her. "Do you want me to get Ronica? Or one of the girls?"

"Oh ... any one of them will do," she said in a thready voice. The room was beginning to swim again. "Oh, and get Cedric ... he'll know the name of that baby." She laid her head back against the chair and willed the shifting colors which descended upon her from behind her eyelids to carry her away to someplace else ... it didn't matter where.

Hollie woke some time later and was surprised to see that it was apparently early evening. She wondered how it had come to pass that she had fallen asleep so early in the day. She was in a chair in her sitting room, covered with a quilt.

Strange. Something wasn't quite right.

She tilted her head toward the window, from which a somber gray light filtered through the drapes, and was surprised to see her sister-in-law there on the window seat. "Ronica," Hollie said, and her voice sounded strange, tired, in her own ears, "is everything alright? Where is Owan?"

"He's right here. He's fine," Ronica replied. "Oh, Hollie," she moaned, "it's so sad, isn't it?"

Alarmed, Hollie said, "What is? Ronica, what's wrong?"

"Why, Cedric, of course. Oh, poor dear," she looked at Hollie tenderly, "Smead told me that the news had made you quite daft."

Hollie threw the quilt to the floor, and stood unsteadily to her feet, holding her hand out for balance. "Esselte!" she cried, and staggered out of the room, headed for the stairs.

Ronica waited until she had left, and then called after her, "Hollie! Wait!" Then she walked over to Owan's cradle, picked up the little boy, and held him in her arms, cooing softly, "There, there, little one ... someone will take care of you, if your mother can't. Someone will always love you."

Hollie reeled down the hallway to Smead's study, did not find him there, and ran on to the dining hall. Finding the room about half full of nearly silent people, she cried again, "Esselte!"

From the center of a little knot of people, Smead hastily rose and said, "My Lady." He pushed his way through the gathered mourners to where she waited, weaving unsteadily, breathlessly. Sir Willum and a boy that she almost recognized, and one that she didn't, followed Smead to where Hollie stood.

Her eyes wild, desperate, she stared feverishly at Smead, trying to understand. "Esselte, is it true?" He gazed back into her eyes sadly. "Is Cedric dead?"

"Yes, my dear ... I'm afraid he's gone."

She grabbed the front of his robes with her fists, and Smead thought for a moment that she was going to lift him completely off the floor, but then all of her frantic strength drained from her arms as fast as it had come, and she began to whimper, her lower lip quaking uncontrollably. "Esselte," she whispered, "it can't be true, can it?"

121

He gathered her into his arms and let her cry then, as the silent mourners, miserable and ashamed, walked quietly from the hall and headed back to their own places.

Chapter Twenty-Four

Will stood in the courtyard beneath Piper's window, wondering whether to call up to her or not. He was miserable, of course, but she was inconsolable. Still, he did not want to leave without making things right with her, at least as right as he could make them.

He considered just going ... but could not. Reaching down for a handful of pebbles, he tossed them up to her ledge, where they skittered noisily into her room. A moment later, she appeared at the window, looking silently down upon him. Her face was red and puffy, and she did not look particularly lovely. But still, Will's heart went out to her, full of sadness and longing.

"Come down and walk with me in the garden," he said.

She hesitated a moment, then said heavily, "I'm so tired, Will. And it's cold."

"I need to see you," he persisted.

"I don't know why," she said dubiously.

"Will ye come down?"

A moment's pause. "No, Will."

Will looked around the courtyard, agitated, unsure. In the gloom of dusk the familiar shapes cast shadows that looked grotesque, disturbed. And it *was* cold.

"Well, can I come up there to yer room, then?"

She looked down at him, thinking, sad, then gave one curt nod.

"I'm comin' up."

A few stealthy, heart-pounding steps later and he was slipping through the rooms that Haldamar and Ronica Tenet shared with their family and into Piper's chamber; she had left the door ajar for him. He glided into the room and shut the door behind him as silently as he could.

Piper stood in the darkness of her bedroom with her head downturned and her back to Will. Not looking in his direction, she said, "Uncle Cedric's dead."

"I know," he whispered, wondering what kind of greeting that might be. "Will yer parents hear us talkin'?" She shook her head no, and he figured she probably knew.

"Will we ever be safe again?" she asked softly.

"I don't know." He took a step closer to her. "Piper, might I put my arms around ye?"

"If you want to."

He took her into his embrace, burying his face in her hair, breathing in her scent, loving the way she felt in his arms. After a moment she returned the embrace, holding him close to her.

"Ye're not cryin'," Will observed, and berated himself for saying such a stupid thing out loud.

"No." She pressed her cheek against his. "I'm about cried out, I guess."

"Oh," Will said, feeling guilty. "I'm sorry."

"I'm tired," she said halfheartedly. "Can we sit down?"

"Uh ... sure. Of course."

She sat on the edge of her bed and patted a spot next to her, where he sat obediently.

She breathed in, and exhaled slowly. "Do you know how many boys wanted to court me before you came to Castle Thraill?"

"No. Lots, I suppose."

"Lots."

A moment of silence passed between them as Will wondered where this conversation might be heading. But he was grateful that at least there was a conversation.

"I never was interested in any of them. And then … you came, and decided to win my heart." She looked at him openly, transparently displaying the heart that Willum had won. "I never had a chance. You are stronger than I am, and you have taken me by force, like the wind, like a tempest. I am helpless. I am … broken."

"Piper—"

"You are planning to go and fight the dragon. The dragon that killed Uncle Cedric. The dragon that kills everybody." She didn't wait for his response, but continued calmly, "I am going to make a fool of myself now."

"Piper—"

"Will, I beg you to change your mind. Stay here with me. Marry me. I will do anything I can do to make you happy, to make you … stay."

Willum looked around the dimly lit bedchamber, seeing the dressing table, silky gowns draped over chairs, pretty things hanging on walls. He recognized some of the many flowers he had given her so long ago, which had been dried and hung upside-down on little pegs around the room. Will had often wondered what it looked like in Piper's bedroom, and had occasionally imagined romantic interludes taking place here, but he had never imagined that the one time he would finally see the inside of Piper's room would be when he was saying goodbye.

"The reason I came ... was to tell ye that ... I love ye. That there ain't nothin' I'd wish to do besides bein' yer husband and raisin' a batch of little ones with ye. And if ... if ye'll wait for me, and if God sees fit ... when I get home again, that's just what I'll do."

Despite her assertion that she was cried out, a fresh stream of tears appeared on Piper's cheeks. Will saw, and gently laid his hand on hers. They sat like that for several minutes, both of them staring mutely at the floor in their shared anguish.

"Will...?" she whispered.

He turned his gaze from the floor to her face, and found her sad eyes regarding him with something inexpressible. Not hope ... or hopelessness ... but something that was both at once.

"If you wish ... you may marry me now."

It was a moment before the significance of her offer sunk in, and when it did, Will was shocked—shocked and flattered. For a fleeting second, he was tempted to accept. It was, after all, what he had dreamed about while he was drifting off to sleep for most of the nights of the past year. But then, regretfully, he said, "No ... we can't do that."

A fresh wound of rejection appeared in Piper's eyes. She whispered sadly, "I thought you said ... that you wanted to marry me."

"More than anything," Will said earnestly. "But, not even takin' into account that we'd probably get caught by your mother ... it just wouldn't be fair to ye."

"It's me who made the offer," she said, her face red with humiliation.

"Piper, my love ... if I come home again, I'll beg yer father to let me marry ye the first night I get back. But ... what if we were to ...ye know—" his cheeks brightened as well, "—and say, ye were to come along with child, and then I never returned. Ye'd be shamed. Ye'd be dishonored."

"I don't care," she said, but she already knew she was not going to win this discussion.

"And ... if I was to take such a precious gift from ye, and not come back for ye ... well, then it just wouldn't be fair to the man who *does* marry ye someday, neither." His heart grew heavy at the idea of somebody else marrying Piper.

"Then why are you here anyway, Willum of Blythecairne?" Piper demanded crossly, her voice rising slightly.

"I just ... wanted ye to know how much I do love ye, and to ask ye, if ye would ... to wait awhile for me before findin' somebody else to love."

"Go away. I am so tired. I'm tired of dragons, and I'm tired of death, and I'm tired of *you*, Will. I'm tired."

Will looked at her wistfully for a moment, longing to kiss her, longing to hold her in his arms one last time. The thought occurred to him that he might take by force that which she had just offered freely, and he was horrified to recognize it, and sorry for being the kind of man who could think such a thought. "All right," he said softly.

Piper did not look at him as he slipped to the door, paused to gaze at her for one last remorseful moment, and then was gone. She lay on her back, exhausted, staring at the ceiling, so tired, unable to sleep. At last she drifted off for a while, but her sleep was fitful and her dreams dark, and she kept waking up every hour or so, to ache, to mourn, to long, to suffer.

Chapter Twenty-Five

Hollie sat before her looking glass the next morning, and she thought she understood. Her husband was dead. Cedric was dead. He was never coming back again. She would never see him again. He would not help her raise Owan. He was dead.

She looked at the woman in the mirror, whose beauty mocked the pain that Hollie was feeling. She watched the woman for a moment, who stared blankly back at her, stared at her stupidly like some kind of imbecile.

She picked up a knife and began to cut, and felt some small measure of satisfaction as the long golden curls dropped silently to the floor. Now the woman would not be so smug. Now she would know the pain that Hollie felt. Now they could share. They were sisters in Hollie's pain. Hollie wondered who the woman was, and why she kept on staring back at her.

She heard the baby begin to cry, and rose to go to him, still clutching the knife.

ſ

Will heard the baby crying, and felt hopeful. Must be Hollie was in her room.

There would be no sendoff for Will like there had been for Roarke. No lines of tearful people, no pats on the back or prayers. Will had not told anyone he was leaving today, not even King of the Dragon or Master

Smead. Just Piper. But he wished to see Hollie before he left, to get her blessing, to say goodbye.

He knocked respectfully on Hollie's door, but there was no answer. The baby kept on crying, though, and Will grew alarmed. He tried the latch of the door, found it unlocked, pushed it open.

A woman stood over Owan's cradle, staring down at him, brandishing a long knife. The woman wore a loose-fitting dressing gown, with blonde hair unevenly hacked off, and a couple of trickles of blood running down her neck. With a horrified shock of recognition, Will realized that the woman was Hollie.

She heard the door open and looked up at him, her blue eyes vacant. But then she said in a halting voice, as if she had forgotten how to speak and was just recalling how to formulate words, "You're ... you're Will."

"Hollie! What have ye done?" he asked, dismayed.

"What ... have I done?" she repeated, and began to weep. "What ... have I done?"

Will hurried over to her and gently removed the knife from her hand, tossing it to the floor. He checked the baby and found that Owan was unharmed, and then put his arms around the trembling woman.

"Will ... have you heard?" she sobbed. "Cedric ... Cedric is...."

"Yes, Hollie, I've heard," he said, hoping that he was being comforting. He stroked her back and patted her shoulders. "We're all sad right now."

She did not respond, but continued to cry. She leaned against him, sobbing, and the sounds of her cries and the baby's soon brought Ronica Tenet to the door, wearing a concerned expression on her face.

"Sir Willum! What are you—?" Then she saw Hollie, saw the golden hair lying on the floor, the blood on her neck. She shook her head sadly and said, "I should tend to the baby."

"Aye, that'd help," Will agreed.

Ronica gathered up Owan and bustled him out of the room, leaving Will alone with the heartbroken woman. Hollie continued crying, until Will's tunic was soaked through by her tears. He stood patiently holding her, letting her weep, until his lower back began to ache. He said, "Do ye think we might sit for a bit, Hollie?"

"Oh, Will, I'm so sorry," Hollie said, slowly coming to her senses. She removed herself from his embrace, and sat down shakily on her window seat.

"What's happened to my hair?"

"I believe ye did that to yerself," Will said cautiously.

"Oh," she said. "It's just as well, I suppose." A thoughtful look came over her. "I will mourn, and wear a black veil, until my heart mends, if it ever does. By that time, it should have grown back." Then she remembered again that Roarke was dead, and began to cry, covering her face with her hands.

ꝼ

Will finally made his way down to the stables about midday, after deciding that, in fact, Hollie was going to recover from the deep sickness that had accompanied her grief. He determined that the best thing he could

131

do to save the lives and the sanity of the people that he loved would be to go and kill the dragon as quickly as he could.

He stepped into the barn and froze in his tracks, startled. "I was starting to wonder if maybe you had changed your mind," Piper said. She did not smile.

"I, ah, I have to go," Will said lamely.

"I know. And I will ride with you for a bit."

Her face was no longer red and puffy (though she had dark circles under her eyes), and her long auburn hair had been brushed. She wore an olive-green riding coat that was a particular favorite of Will's. He thought that she looked as lovely as he had ever seen her.

He walked over to where he had stowed his gear, and finished packing his horse, while she watched him, arms crossed, silent, pensive.

"Well," Willum said, indicating that he was ready to go.

"Wait."

He looked at her.

"I want to apologize for last night." She took his hand and looked a little uncomfortable. "Not for what I offered to you—I would offer that again. But how I behaved when you turned me down. I'm sorry about that."

"It's all right."

"Let me kiss you," Piper said, and Will hungrily obliged. They clung to each other for a deep, warm moment, as the horses stamped in their stalls. "Come home to me again, Willum of Blythecairne," Piper said, barely audible. *I will if I can*, he thought, but he looked into her eyes and nodded.

ſ

King of the Dragon scuttled to the apartments of Haldamar Tenet and his family, opened the door without knocking, and walked in.

"Welcome, Your Highness," Haldamar said genuinely. "A pleasure to see you again."

"Welcome, yerself," the King said kindly. "Is yer Piper aboot anywheres?"

"Yes, I think so. Jesi, will you go and fetch your sister?"

The little kobold said, "It's really Sir Willum what I'm lookin' fer. But I cain't find him nowheres, an' I figgered that yer Piper would have a line on 'im." A moment later, a solemn and unsmiling Paipaerria Tenet reported to her father. He noticed her demeanor and made a quick mental note to ask her about it after the King was gone. He addressed her: "Piper, the King is looking for Sir Will. Do you know where he is?"

"He's gone," she said simply. "Gone to fight the dragon."

"He is?" Haldamar said, rising from his chair. "Does Smead know?"

"Not yet."

"When did he leave?"

"This afternoon. He told me not to tell anybody until I was asked."

King of the Dragon's eyes flared bright red, and he rose to his tallest possible height. "He didn't tell *me*?" he demanded. "What was the idear o' *that*?" Piper shrugged noncommittally.

"Who's he think I am, anyways? *Prince* o' th' Dragon? No, I ain't! I'm th' *King* o' th' Dragon, what Sir Willum called me hisself, an' he never shoulda gone off an' left me behind! He'll *need* me!" Pointing to Haldamar, he ordered, "Get me a 'oss sattled up. I got t' foller 'im."

Piper said, "Daddy, Will asked that we make sure that the King stays here."

Placatingly, Haldamar said to him, "That sounds like wisdom to me, Your Highness. You might get lost trying to follow Sir Will."

"Lost?" the kobold said angrily. "Well, if ye won't give me a 'oss, then I'll jest hafta foller 'im afoot."

"But what will you eat?" asked Jesi, who had come back into the room with Piper.

"What'd I eat when I lived alone at th' dragon's cave? I made do."

"Your Highness," Piper tried, "please don't go. Will just wants to protect you."

"Aye, I get it," the King said, and his eyes dimmed a bit to an orange-red. "But who's goin' t' pertect *him*?" Without another word, the little gray kobold turned and trotted from the room. He stopped at the kitchen for a slab of cold beef, which he stuffed into a pocket of his trousers, and then trotted from the castle, through the gate, and into the snow-covered fields. Sniffing the air for a moment, his nostrils twitching alertly, he made a decision and began jogging eastward.

Chapter Twenty-Six

Hollie woke the next morning, and knew immediately that Roarke was dead. She reached up and felt the ragged stubble on her head, and knew that she had done it. She remembered that Roarke's sister had taken care of Owan throughout the night, and she knew that it was because Ronica had feared Hollie was insane.

She supposed she *had* been insane, yesterday maybe, the day before certainly. She toyed with the idea of being ashamed for her conduct, but decided that it wasn't important. She was sane now, as far as she knew, and she had the rest of her life to begin living. She had a son to provide for, and decisions to make, she supposed. Though she could not think of any decisions that had to be made.

Maybe later.

For now, she needed to take care of herself, so that she could take care of Owan. Her arms, her breasts, ached for her son, a tangible pain.

She needed to get up, get out of bed. Find a black gown with a black veil; she thought she had one that would suffice. Find Owan. Get some breakfast. One step at a time. One step at a time.

She wished to live a life that would honor the memory of her husband—his nobility, his strength, his wisdom, his frailty. She had spent enough time being insane.

Rising from her bed, she made her way over to the looking glass, and stared with dismay at her own reflection. "My ... aren't you a sight," she said to the Hollie in the mirror. She found the knife that she had used yesterday, and quickly tried to finish the job of cutting her hair as evenly as she could. It still looked pretty bad, but at least it should grow back with some kind of uniformity.

As she dressed, she recalled the conversation she had had with Willum a day earlier, after he had found her standing over the baby's cradle.

He had let her cry for awhile, but finally had said to her, "Hollie ... it just wouldn't be right."

She had looked at him then with a question in her sad eyes, but had said nothing.

"Lord Roarke's whole life, just about, was spent tryin' to help others, and doin' whatever he knew to be the right thing to do." Will struggled to say what he had to say politely. "Lord Roarke paid a great price for yer life, tryin' to bless ye. Now, it was a little bit selfish, maybe, because ye *were* the most beautiful woman he ever seen. But mostly, it was for *yer* benefit, not his.

"And now ye're the mother of his child, and the Lady of a whole big estate. I might be steppin' in a bit over my head here, but I think if Lord Roarke was here to tell ye what to do next ... he'd tell ye to spend yer life carin' for yer boy, and carin' for yer people. To spend yer life givin', like he done. Not to be feelin' too sorry for yerself. Thankin' God for all the good things that He's gave ye, and not complainin' too much about what He's took away.

"Anyway, that's what I think. I'm sorry if I've overspoke my piece." She had understood. Nodded, unable to speak.

Will had continued, "Remember Roarke's kindness. Remember his gentleness and his generosity. Remember Roarke's wisdom. Remember his faith in God, and how he trusted Him, no matter how things looked. And say to yerself, 'Why, Hollie, ye should try to be like that, too.'"

He had sighed and concluded, "Well, I guess that's all I got to say. I hope ye'll be all right." He had looked at her tenderly then, and something in his look reminded Hollie of the first night she had served Will and Cedric at Kenndt's table.

She was amazed when she thought of how much had happened since that day, what tremendous upheavals of change had occurred in their lives.

"Thank you, Will," she had managed. "I will be all right. I will."

And so, she supposed, she was. She fixed the veil in its place and headed toward Ronica's rooms, to see if she could find Owan.

ɾ

Esselte Smead saw the black-shrouded figure gliding through the hallway toward the dining hall, and immediately recognized the form of the Lady Hollie. He held up his hand in apology for interrupting the conversation in which he was engaged, then stood and walked over to her.

"My Lady," he said uneasily, "are you well?"

Hollie reached out and took his hand. "I'm better today, Master Smead, and I believe I am in my right mind."

He could see her smiling weakly from within the fabric of her veil, and felt a profound sense of relief. A smile crossed his own round, red face in reply. "I am happy to see you about, my dear."

"I guess I put you all through a fright the past couple of days, didn't I? I am very sorry."

"We were all very shaken by the sad news," Smead protested. "No one thinks any less of you for … faltering."

"Thank you." She changed the subject. "I was trying to find Owan. I thought he was with Ronica, but she's not at home." She was weak from hunger, beginning to tremble. "Maybe if I eat something first … then would you help me find my baby?"

"Yes, oh my! Come sit, and I will serve you."

"Thank you," Hollie said softly, accepting his kindness gratefully.

Smead bustled off to the kitchen to fetch some breakfast, and Hollie became conscious of the others in the room lowering their voices and stealing glances in her direction. She decided to lift her veil—not so far that they could see what had happened to her hair, but enough so that they could see her face. When she did so, the other diners began standing up and approaching her, first one, then another, then all of them, offering their condolences and expressing their sorrow for her loss. For their shared loss.

Hollie accepted the sympathy of her friends, somehow understanding that they needed to give as much as she needed to receive. Many of them had known Cedric Roarke far longer than she had, and their sense of bereavement was genuine.

Smead came back in with a steaming platter of eggs and bacon, but before he got all the way back to Hollie's seat, he was detained by two young men. Hollie thought she recognized them from somewhere, though she could tell they weren't from Castle Thraill. She thought she heard one of them say, "Should I tell her now?" but she saw Smead shake his head no.

"Esselte," she said, as Smead placed the platter in front of her, "who are those boys?"

"They are from Ester," he said, not directly lying.

"Do they want to tell me something?"

"There will be time for that later," Smead said. "Another time."

Her heart seemed to jump in her breast, and she said, "Oh, no—it's not more bad news, is it?"

"I don't want you to be troubled by it today."

She took his hand and said, "Esselte, if I don't find out what it is now, my imagination will be running away with me, God knows where, until I do. I don't know that I could bear it! Have them come to me."

Smead wore a pained look on his swarthy face. "I really must—"

"Please."

After a moment's indecision, Smead beckoned to the two boys, who had been watching. They walked over to Hollie's place at the table, and bowed humbly.

"May I present Alan, son of Lord Poppleton of Ester, and his squire Brette," Smead said.

"Alan … Poppleton. We have met before, I think?" Hollie said uncertainly.

"Yes, my Lady, back when you first came to the castle."

"Oh, yes. But—" she tried to remember something Cedric had said about Alan. "Wait. You went to do battle with the dragon. And you have survived. I don't understand."

"My Lady—"

"It must have been you who brought back word of Cedric's death."

"Yes, my Lady. Forgive me for having borne such ill tidings to you."

Hollie looked worried, confused. "How did you escape?"

"That ... ah ... that's what we need to tell you," Alan said, casting a nervous glance at Brette and Smead.

"What?" she said. The room was beginning to spin again, and the outer ranges of her periphery were starting to turn black.

"The dragon gave us a message to give you," Alan said guiltily.

"The ... dragon...."

"I'm sorry, my Lady. Maybe we shouldn't—"

"Tell me," she said, and swallowed. She clutched Smead's hand tightly, her knuckles white as bone.

"The dragon said, 'Hollie, come.'"

An abrupt laugh escaped Hollie's lips. "The dragon said—" She looked at Smead helplessly, with a wild fear loose in her eyes.

Alan, thinking that Hollie was asking him to repeat himself, said, "'Hollie, come.'"

"'Hollie, come,'" she echoed. *Hollie, come.*

Suddenly she knew. She knew that she would never be safe. Owan would never be safe. Piper, Jesi, Smead, Helen—they would never be safe, as long as the dragon lived. *Hollie, come.* It would follow her, wherever she tried to hide, and everyone that she left behind would be in danger, because it would track her, hunt her, stalk her, for the rest of her days. *Hollie, come.*

There was a sound like rushing wind in her ears, like a waterfall, and the darkness in the room grew until it covered everything and there was silence.

Silence, but for the words *Hollie, come.*

Chapter Twenty-Seven

Porcatie had found his way back to the forest that surrounded the headwaters of the Eldric River. Confounded by his own cowardice, he shunned contact with other men, or at least he would have if he had seen any. It seemed that everyone who had inhabited Solemon was either dead or removed to Ruric's Keep or Lenidor. Porcatie was lonely, starving, and had seen enough of terrifying death to make him just a little mad.

He had been unable to trap or kill any wild game and had been reduced to eating pine nuts and scrabbling around in the earth for edible roots. He considered butchering Brette's horse, which was also struggling to find suitable forage, but he decided that he wasn't quite that desperate yet. Without a horse, he might never leave the forest again, and he wasn't sure he wanted to resign himself to that fate, not yet.

ɼ

"Oh, no ... I've done it again, haven't I?" Hollie croaked to Jesi Tenet.

"It's all right, Aunt Hollie. You've had a terrible time. You just fainted, and needed to get some rest."

From the shadows in her room, Hollie could tell that it must be evening, and she knew she had slept the whole day, and had not cared for her baby again.

"Owan," she said.

"He's all right," Jesi said. "Mother has been happy to have him. And Piper's helped a little bit."

Hollie felt shamed that she was being such a poor mother, but then remembered Alan Poppleton's message to her. *Hollie, come.* It was almost as if she could hear the dragon itself speaking the words. She was glad that Ronica was content to have Owan.

"Oh, Jesi … this is hard," Hollie sighed.

Jesi smiled encouragingly at her aunt. "Alan was so sorry to see that what he told you made you faint. He felt just terrible about it."

"You spoke to him?" Hollie asked idly, not really very interested, but a little curious at the familiarity Jesi apparently shared with young Poppleton.

"Yes, the last thing that Uncle Cedric ever told me was, if Alan Poppleton came here again, to listen to what he had to say."

Sorrowfully, Hollie murmured, "I'm not even sure I remember what the last thing Cedric ever told me was." She could probably figure it out if she tried very hard to concentrate … but everything was so confused right now.

"Aunt Hollie … you haven't heard it yet," Jesi said carefully.

"Yes, I suppose that when I get to Iesuchristi's country, I'll see him again," she said without conviction.

"No, I mean you haven't heard his last words to you yet. Down here, I mean."

Hollie shook her head slightly and closed her eyes. She did not understand.

Jesi explained, "Alan says he's very sorry that he told you what the dragon said, but forgot to tell you what Uncle Cedric said. He wrote to you—Uncle Cedric did—before he went to fight the dragon."

"He ... wrote to me?" Fresh tears blurred Hollie's eyes.

"Yes. I have it right here."

"Will you ... will you read it to me?" Hollie blinked the tears away as best as she could.

"Do you want to break the seal?" Jesi offered. Breaking the seal was always the most exciting part of receiving a letter for Jesi, even better than the contents. She had received four letters in her life, an astounding number.

"No, you go ahead."

Jesi gingerly pulled the parchment open, a few crumbled bits of sealing wax dropping onto her lap. "Are you ready?" she asked.

Hollie nodded.

"This is it:

> *To Hollie Roarke, my beloved, my greatly beloved:*
>
> *Knowing and loving you has been the greatest honor a man could ever have. Thank you. I thank God that He allowed us these glorious days.*
>
> *Even though I shall not see you again, trust His goodness.*
>
> *With all my love, Cedric*

"He signed it himself," Jesi concluded.

Hollie took a moment to compose herself before she attempted to speak. She breathed in, breathed out. *These glorious days.* She was not sure whether to be grateful or to be angry, with Cedric or with God. "Jesi ... would you leave me alone for a few minutes?"

"Will you be all right?"

She nodded. "And could you please bring Owan to me? I need to see my baby boy."

Jesi handed Hollie the letter and left the room. Hollie pressed the parchment to her lips and closed her eyes.

ʃ

Porcatie saw the rider approaching from the west, saw the saddlebags bulging behind his legs, wondered if they were full of food. He wondered if the rider would share. Maybe Porcatie should warn him about the dragon. No, that was stupid. If somebody was coming across the northern plain, west to east, then he already knew about the dragon.

Maybe he should just waylay him, rob him. Kill him? Porcatie debated for a moment. The dragon would certainly kill him anyway, so what would be the difference? Then Porcatie would have two horses; he could eat one, and save one to ride back to ... to ride back to.... Where would he go? Where would he ever go that he would dare to show his face again, coward and murderer and thief that he was? Porcatie began to cry pitifully, feeling enormously sorry for himself.

The rider drew nearer, and still Porcatie did not know what to do. Hide? No ... no food then! Need food. What to do? Porcatie heard a strangled cry of confused frustration rising in the air around him, realized it was his own voice, knew that there was no longer any point in hiding, and stumbled out of the trees into the open, waving his arms. "Rider! Help! Help me!"

ʃ

King of the Dragon jogged along the trail that Sir Willum's horse left in the snow-dusted plain. He couldn't run nearly so fast as the horse went, but he made up for it partly by continuing to run for as long as there was enough light for him to make out the path. Then he would sit on the ground, nibble a bit of beef, and doze until the light returned.

It wasn't too cold, not since he had started wearing clothes. He thought wistfully that he wished he had known more about clothes earlier in his life; it would have saved him from many a shivering night. Well, never too late to learn.

He was almost out of beef. He hoped it wasn't too much farther to the dragon. But he figured that, even if he had to suffer a couple of days with nothing to eat, there was a feast of dragon meat ahead of him! Once he used his magic to kill this one, there would be enough meat for a year, maybe longer if he didn't gorge too much.

As he dozed, the little kobold dreamed about killing the dragon, and what magic words he might use. He figured that, once he killed this dragon—which apparently no man could do—then everyone would know about his powers. And then, maybe he wouldn't just be King of the Dragon. Maybe the human folk would make him King of the Whole World. Then wouldn't them stinkers Tilda and Vesta be sorry!

He only hoped he could catch up to his friend Sir Willum soon enough to protect him from the dragon. Sir Willum didn't have any magic.

Chapter Twenty-Eight

Will saw the emaciated man stumbling out of the forest, arms flailing, crying for help, and was a little unnerved. He had not seen very many men in the past two weeks—none at all in the last four days—and this one looked more like a tattered wraith than a man. Will didn't pull back on the reins, but Starlight shied away from the shrieking apparition anyway, and Will had to wrestle to keep him from bucking.

After satisfying himself that the man was crying for help, and not trying to frighten him away, Will steadied his horse and rode toward him. "How can I help ye, friend?"

The man ran up to Will, clinging to his leg and weeping. "You're a knight, aren't you? Do you have food?"

"Aye, I'll feed ye. Do ye have a camp? Are there more of ye?"

"No, it's just me. Just me and my horse. We're awful hungry."

"Well, lead me to yer camp, and I'll bide with ye for the night." Will dismounted so that he could walk with the man. "My name is Willum, friend. What're ye called?"

"My name was Porcatie, back when I was a man. But I'm all alone now, and my horse don't call me anything, and I'm less than a man now, less than I used to be anyway. Though I don't suppose I was ever so much of a man as I thought I was. God, you don't have something you could give me to eat while we walk, do you?"

"Would a piece of jerky help?" Willum said, and produced one.

Porcatie grabbed the dried lump of meat greedily and began chewing it, chewing it, softening it enough so that he could swallow. The exertion of gnawing the jerky was enough to keep him from talking, as he led Will and Starlight into the trees.

Will asked, "Do ye know about the dragon?"

A hunted look darkened Porcatie's eyes, and it seemed as if he ducked his head. He nodded, though, and swallowed the last of the jerky. "You're Sir Willum the Bold, aren't you?"

Will answered, "I been called that, I guess."

"I was with your master, the last night he was alive—with him and Keltur and two boys that he sent home."

Will paused to digest that bit of information, and though he had many questions he would have asked, he settled on one. "We're close to the dragon, then?"

"Two days more to the east, if you ride steady." Porcatie liked the look of this young fellow, and was both impressed and shamed by Will's apparent courage. "Don't go."

"I wish," Will ruefully replied. He started unpacking his cookware from his saddlebags and preparing a meal for the two of them to share. Porcatie watched him blankly as he worked.

Will noticed him standing there and said, "Ye could help by gatherin' a bit of wood for a fire, if it ain't too much trouble."

"Sorry," Porcatie mumbled, and stirred himself to action. Once again he felt the sting of humiliation, of shame, and once again he was tempted to take a bough and bring it crashing down on Willum's head as he knelt over the pan. He was only going to be killed by the dragon anyway.

ʃ

He had followed Sir Willum's trail southward from Castle Thraill to Lauren, skirting the northern edge of the town rather than showing himself openly on the streets. He had forded the Strait Elles and then picked up Will's scent again east of town, following the King's Road then to the Strait Penne, and crossing a little wooden bridge that led to, apparently, nowhere. But he could tell that that was the direction Sir Willum had gone; the smell of his horse had still been in the air. King of the Dragon had always liked the smell of Will's horse Starlight. Not for eating. Just for smelling.

He had followed Will's path over the Sayl Mountains, where he had almost lost the scent, but kept on heading eastward, and when he descended the other side, there it was again. Then he had jogged for two days across the windswept plains, and had finally run out of food. But in the distance ahead of him, he thought he could faintly make out the form of a rider on a horse, and knew that he was almost caught up.

At daybreak, while Will was making breakfast and puttering around in his camp, King of the Dragon roused himself immediately and starting trotting toward him again. He jumped and shouted a couple of times, but Will did not notice him across the distance. Even if he had been able to hear the shouts, he probably would not have been able to see the little kobold against the long silvery-gray backdrop of the plains. Will mounted Starlight and started off again toward the east, and the distance between them once more grew greater than it had been at dawn.

King of the Dragon could still see Sir Willum clearly by the time Will arrived at the forest, and he watched with dismay as the other figure appeared from out of the shadow of the trees. He watched Sir Willum dismount and follow the other one into the darkness, and cursed his short legs. He would not be able to catch up again, not today. If Will had camped

151

out in the open, then maybe sometime in the middle of the night … but not now.

ꭇ

Porcatie found a large, stout branch and gauged its heft. He visualized bringing it down on the back of Will's neck, and cringed. A silent debate raged in his head, between the part of him that still had a conscience, could still feel shame, and the part that was just craven and desperate and hungry.

It took both of his hands to lift the branch above his head; it was that heavy. His elbows and knees felt weak. *Just do it if you're going to do it*, he told himself testily. The dragon was going to kill him anyway.

Aren't you any kind of a man? he derided himself. When he asked himself that silent question, though, he meant that if he were any kind of a man, he would just walk back in and club the boy over the skull with the bough. But his conscience quickly pricked him: If he were any kind of a man, he would ride with Sir Willum to face the dragon, and die an honorable death.

But the place beyond the reach of Porcatie's conscience was tired of feeling guilty, tired of feeling cowardly. He set his mouth in a grim line, and took another practice swing with the club.

Climbing over the brush back toward his camp, he saw Will from between the trees, kneeling on the ground trying to kindle the fire. *What are you thinking about?* he demanded himself incredulously. He thought he should probably gather a few more branches or sticks to carry back in along with this bough, but he did not.

Porcatie scowled.

Walking back into the campsite, he hoisted the club up on his right shoulder, and stepped closer to Will, who was bent low to the earth, blowing on the small flame he had created.

Stepping next to the boy, he lifted the branch from his shoulder, paused for a beat, then bent and laid it down on the ground beside Will. Unsure whether to laugh or cry, he slumped to the dirt, sitting with his back against a tree.

Will looked at the branch, and said, "That's a nice big piece of wood. Can ye maybe bring me a few smaller ones to use, too?"

Porcatie said in a feeble voice, "I don't think so."

Will looked at the man, saw the confusion in his eyes, and said, "Don't worry about it. I'll take care of ye, and get some food in yer belly soon. Just rest."

Chapter Twenty-Nine

Hollie looked up from where she held Owan against her bosom. Esselte Smead had just rapped politely upon her doorsill, peering in expectantly.

"Thank you for coming, Master Smead. I have a request of you."

"Anything, my dear." He was encouraged to see that she was clear-eyed and alert, and showed no sign of the lingering unsteadiness that Smead feared would be her fate.

"Now that Cedric has died … please forgive me if I have misunderstood. Now that Cedric is gone … am I still the Lady of Thraill? Are you still my steward?"

Smead's face, which was normally quite red, turned a couple of shades more crimson. "My Lady … I don't know how to tell you."

She favored him with a resigned smile. "More unhappy news, I see. Don't fear, Esselte. I don't believe that I will lose control this time. I am becoming reconciled to the idea of this season of my life not going entirely as I would have wished."

"I'll just tell you, then … I had hoped that Lord Roarke himself would have told you, but I perceive that he has not." He took a deep breath. "Under the terms of his will … *I* am now the Lord of Thraill. Subject to King Ruric's approval." He did not mention the fact that Marta Dressler might have a claim on half the estate as well.

"Oh, my," Hollie murmured. Then she brightened perceptibly, and smiled at Smead. "What a wise choice. Does Ronica know?"

155

"The question hasn't come up yet, though she was aware of her brother's will in time past."

"And, ah ... what does that make *me*?"

He looked at her awkwardly. "You ... are my guest." He hurriedly added, "And not only that—you are the mother of my heir." She looked at him curiously.

He continued, "Lord Roarke asked me to name Owan as my heir, since I have no heir of my own. I agreed, of course."

"Well ... so much information," she mused. "At least Owan will be well-provided for."

"As will you, my dear! Anything you ever desire, for as long as you live, I will most happily provide." Hollie was slightly taken aback by the earnestness of this profession.

She regarded him thoughtfully for a moment, and then said, "If I were Lady and you were my steward, I would just ask you how to do what I need done, and you would do it. But since you are Lord and I am your guest ... I have no authority to command. But I do beg you, Esselte—please grant my request."

"You have no need to beg, Hollie. You will always be my Lady, in whatever realm you wish to be." He looked extremely embarrassed. "Anything you want, please just ask."

"Thank you, Esselte. In fact ... I was going to ask for some money."

"Do you have a need that is not being supplied here at the castle?" Smead wondered. "Forgive me! That's not my business, of course. Any amount you need, up to half of the treasury, shall be yours."

"I need to create a monument to Cedric. Something of my own design, my own way."

"A monument," Smead echoed guardedly. "An admirable request. Will you require the help of an artist? An engineer?"

"Just the money, for now. How much would it cost in eglons to make something like the fountain in the garden? The stone dragon?"

Smead calculated, "I believe Ronica commissioned that sculpture for twenty eglons. Or perhaps it was twenty-five. It was some time ago."

"Then, may I please have fifty? If that isn't too much to ask."

"Not at all. Shall I draw up a draft for you?"

"If I might have the eglons in actual gold pieces ...may I?"

"Certainly," said Smead. He wondered what she was planning, but figured that her reasons were her own. "When do you need them?"

"As soon as possible. Can you have them brought to me?"

"I'll go and get them now, and deliver them myself."

Will and Porcatie shared an uncomfortable breakfast. Porcatie was mostly silent, nervously twitching. Will wondered if there was something seriously wrong with the man—if something other than fright had happened to him. Then he decided that must be the man's nerves were shot, and wondered if he was beyond recovery.

"Will ye ride with me for a day towards Solemon, or do ye wish to stay here?"

Porcatie jerked at the sound of Willum's voice. "No, I believe I'll stay here," he said, his face clouded by the sense of his own disgrace.

"Then what I'll do is take just enough food for today, and breakfast for tomorrow," Will decided. "I'll leave ye the rest. If it happens that I'm allowed to live on after tomorrow, I'll be back and ye can feed me. Then we'll go on back to Castle Thraill together ... mayhap ye can remember yerself there."

"Thank you, Sir Willum," Porcatie said sincerely.

Without wasting any more time on conversation, Will got up from the ground and said, "I've got a hard day's ride ahead of me." He packed just such things on Starlight's flanks as he would completely consume, then mounted up, said, "Goodbye, Porcatie. God's mercy be upon us both," and rode out of the trees and eastward toward the Senns.

ſ

King of the Dragon was hungrier than he thought he would be, so instead of skirting the forest, he followed the path of the two men into the woods. Coming to the camp about midday, he found Porcatie setting Will's food out on the ground, taking inventory. King of the Dragon decided to use some of his magic on the man, to get him to share the food. Not the really powerful magic that he would need to use on the dragon, but just a simple spell to frighten him.

Jumping out of the woods into the clearing, he shouted, "A-a-aahhhhhhhhhhh!" and ran around in a circle. Porcatie, who had never seen a kobold before—had never even imagined one—yelped in terror and went crashing off into the brush.

King of the Dragon sat down on the earth where Porcatie had just been, chortling gleefully. He picked out a few choice morsels and filled his belly. Then he stuffed some jerky into his pockets, got back up off the ground, refreshed, and followed Will's trail back out of the woods, jogging along the aromatic path left by Starlight.

Chapter Thirty

Baniff had been part of Castle Thraill's Dusk Company for over two years, and was weary of guarding the main gate of the castle during the lonely moonlit hours before his compatriot from Dawn Company arrived to relieve him. In two years, he had only had to greet one stranger at the gate. Ever. He wondered why they even bothered to guard the castle at all. Why not just shut the door and put up a sign saying *Come Back Tomorrow* and let everybody sleep?

More than a few times his Dawn Company replacements had come upon him asleep at his post, and once or twice he had been drunk, but no disciplinary action had ever been taken against him, though Dawn Company's captain Hess Boole had been made aware of the issue.

He was dozing again this night, as the Lady Hollie, cloaked and hooded, and wearing a man's leggings instead of a dress, stole past him leading her horse Joy. She marveled that he was able to remain asleep, even with the clacking of the horse's hooves on the cobblestones passing quite closely by him. She had gotten all the way past him and was about to mount and ride off, when her conscience pierced her and she turned back, looking with consternation at the sleeping man. He would undoubtedly get in serious trouble if Hollie disappeared and he had no knowledge of the event, or so she reasoned.

Walking back to where Baniff squatted on the path, snoring, his chin on his chest, she nudged him with her foot, and he almost toppled over in a heap on the ground.

"Who goes? Who goes?" he asked in a panic, blinking his eyes blearily and scrambling to draw his weapon.

"What is your name, sir?" Hollie demanded in a low voice.

"Who are *you*?" he fired back, but then he realized to whom he was speaking. "Lady Hollie! Forgive me! I must've fallen … ill."

"What is your name?"

"It's, ah, Helkin, my Lady," he said, using the name of someone from Dusk Company that he didn't really care for too much. As soon as the lie passed through his lips, he knew that he would be found out if the Lady ever spoke of this to anyone, and hoped he would be allowed to return to private life instead of being thrown in the brig.

"Well, Helkin, I roused you so that you would not be caught asleep at your post. But you must not tell anyone that I passed this way, not until morning. Then you may inform Master Smead. Lord Smead."

"Where are you going?" Baniff asked skeptically, but genuinely curious. Lord Roarke was only recently deceased, so she probably wasn't going to keep a tryst. But she wasn't taking her baby, either. Baniff was perplexed, all the more understandable due to the fact that he was shaking off the effects of liquor-induced slumber.

"That is my own affair," she said. "Don't raise the alarm that I have left, or I will have you disciplined for your failure to watch. Tomorrow you may tell Lord Smead that I have gone … to purchase the monument to my husband that we spoke about."

"That's not true, though, is it?" Baniff said, slyly winking. He felt a little woozy, but not so much that he did not notice the pleasing curve of Hollie's face from within the hood's shadow.

"As a matter of fact, it is." Hollie decided that she did not like this man too much, and regretted having awakened him. She had not been previously exposed to any of Castle Thraill's personnel who were less than honorable, and she was a little shocked, a little offended.

"Well, my Lady, my fine Lady, it's a simple matter for you to buy my silence," he leered drunkenly. "My price is just one kiss." He reached out to grab her arm, but she sidestepped his clumsy move.

Her cheeks flamed with fury. When Cedric heard about this—

Suddenly she realized how alone she was in the world, but did not stop to pity herself. This battle was hers, win or lose—hers alone. "Master Helkin, it's a simple matter for you to purchase your own life. Do not try to touch me again—or when I return, I will have you immediately put in chains!"

"Now, there, Missy, no need to get uppity," he slurred, and reached for her again.

She felt for the bag of fifty gold eglons hanging at her waistline, tore it from her sash, and swung it against the side of Baniff's face, with a thudding chink. He fell in a crumpled heap upon the cobbled path, as the bag split and gold pieces spilled onto the stones.

Oh, no, she thought frantically, kneeling on the path to pick up the coins. She had to spend several precious moments gathering them, and in the end she found only forty-seven. She fought to keep herself from crying, thinking that at any moment the guard might change, and then she would be found out. Before she climbed onto Joy and left the castle, though, she paused long enough to make sure the guard was still breathing. Obeying a sudden impulse, she raised her fingertips to her lips, kissed them, and then pressed them to the unconscious man's cheek.

"There is your price."

Then Hollie mounted her horse and headed southward from the castle, on the path from Thraill to Lauren.

Sir Willum the Bold made camp in a little gully between two sloping mounds on the plain. He ate some cold biscuit, some cold beef, drank some cold water. He thought to himself that, since this was probably his last night on earth, he might at least have a little fire, but then decided against it. If he lit a fire, he might alert the dragon, which might then come upon him prematurely and kill him before he had a chance to strike his blow against it.

He pondered for a bit about the quality of courage … what it was, how it could be fostered, nourished … kept. He could not deny that he was frightened, terribly frightened. But still he was headed forward to his fate, not turning and running away. He considered the idea that maybe he was just foolish … but knew that it was not true.

He wondered what had happened to Porcatie, to leave him the broken shell of a man that he seemed to have become. Will did not want to judge the man too harshly; he didn't know how badly Porcatie had been upset, what terrors he may have suffered. He breathed a quick prayer that it would turn out differently for himself; that no matter what fears he might face on the morrow, he would stand and not run.

Will prayed for Keet, for Keet and Thalia. He prayed for his friends back at Blythecairne, and the new friends he had made in the west. He prayed for Hollie, that her mind would be sound, that she might recover from her sadness. He prayed for Piper, or at least he mentioned her name before the Almighty … but he didn't know what else to say.

He remembered Lord Roarke, and wondered what *he* had prayed, the night before he went to face the dragon for the last time. Was he afraid? Will doubted it. Maybe, though.

"Mighty God ... I don't expect to return from this fight, not unless Ye do somethin' mighty indeed. All I ask is that ye let me strike one blow against the dragon ... to add my stripe to the ones what Lord Roarke already striped it with. That, someday, when the dragon is finally dead, my life helped a little bit ... that I did my part.

"I expect I'll be comin' to see Ye tomorrow for myself. I hope Ye'll be glad to see me. I tried my best, to live like Lord Roarke taught me how. To do justice, and to love mercy. And to be humble in the sight of God. Well, I'm that."

Will rubbed his hands together and blew into his cupped fists. "I hope it's warmer in Yer land than it is here," he said softly. "Sorry—didn't mean to sound like I was complainin'."

ſ

When Kelly of Dawn Company came to relieve Baniff from his post at the castle gate, he thought with disgust that the man was passed out, drunk, yet again. This time he was going to insist that Captain Boole take some kind of action, or else Kelly would go to Esselte Smead himself.

He stalked over to where Baniff lay on the pavement, and gave him a shove with his foot to wake him. When Baniff still didn't rise, though, Kelly bent over and looked at him more closely.

A moment later, he was running back into the guard's quarters, raising the alarm with a shout. The rest of Dawn Company, fresh for duty, as well as the members of Dusk Company who had just been relieved and had not even removed their boots yet, gathered at the main gate, questioning Baniff, who sat groggily, trying to remember what had happened.

Ronica Tenet heard the commotion in the courtyard, and nudged her husband. "Haldamar! Wake up! Something's happened."

He was quickly alert, got up from their bed, threw on a robe, and started for the door.

A moment later she heard him call, "Ronica! Come here!"

She scurried to the door, distressed at the tone in her husband's voice. It was not like Haldamar to call for her when there was potentially trouble about; he had always secretly thought that he was the stronger one of the pair, preferring to think that she needed to be sheltered, protected. Though of course that was not true, Ronica had let him believe it anyway. But this time, he had called for her.

She found Haldamar at the door, bending low over a wicker basket, in which there was a bundle of blankets.

"It's Owan," Haldamar said. "There doesn't seem to be any note."

"Hollie has left him for me," Ronica declared, and Haldamar thought he detected the faintest note of triumph in her voice. "She has killed herself. I saw it in her eyes."

Though Haldamar thought, *No, it couldn't be true*, he feared that his wife may have guessed it. What he said was, "Let me go see about the commotion. I'll be back." He looked at his wife, who had picked up the sleeping baby and pressed him against her bosom. "I hope you're wrong."

Chapter Thirty-One

Hollie had been in Lauren with Cedric several times since they had lived together at Castle Thraill, so she knew her way around town a little bit. Cedric had been happy to show her the landmarks of his youth, though for some reason, they had never visited the farm he had owned when the dragon first struck.

Hollie found the blacksmith of Lauren, a heavily-muscled man named Bulldowne, who seemed to be only a few years older than herself. He was red and sweating from his proximity to the fire, even though the weather outside was bitter and cold. Pausing from his work to wipe his brow with a cloth, he said kindly, "Help you, Missy?"

"Yes ... yes. I believe you fashioned a sword for my husband once?"

"Well, I've made a sword or two in my time. Who's your husband?"

She hesitated just a moment. "He was Lord Roarke of Castle Thraill."

"Why ... are you the Lady Hollie?" he asked with surprise.

She nodded without smiling, and held his gaze.

"I'm awful sorry to hear about your husband," he said. "What a great man he was!"

"Thank you," she murmured. "Did you make his sword?"

"No, I'm Young Bulldowne. My dad, Old Bulldowne—he's the one that made Lord Roarke's sword. I heard that story a hundred times when I was a boy, if I heard it at all."

"Oh...." She seemed uncertain, vulnerable, as if her willpower had been extended beyond its limit.

He saw the hesitance in her eyes, and said gently, "How can I help you, my Lady?"

Looking as if she were slightly confused, Hollie said, "I need ... to have somebody ... make me a sword."

"Well, I could do it, all right. But Old Bulldowne ain't dead yet—he just don't do too much in the way of work any more. Maybe you'd rather talk to him?"

Her eyes flared with hope. "Could I?"

ɼ

Will rode Starlight up the King's Road past the crossbows, looked at the broken machines, and wondered what had happened there. He followed the street northward toward the center of town, and had the curious sensation that he was being watched, but decided that it was just his imagination, just his fear.

The dragon lay in the center of the square, sleeping, immense, colossal, dreadful. Will thought that this must be something like what King of the Dragon had experienced when he had first seen the serpent lying in the Cave of Mendor ... he had never been more afraid in his life. But he dismounted, pointed Starlight back down the street, gave him a slap on his rump, and resolutely drew his sword.

ɼ

Old Bulldowne, a still-muscular man with a shock of wild white hair, said, "Aye ... I remember that sword well. 'Twas the finest one I ever made." He looked at Hollie with a grandfatherly smile. "I heard it was broke, though. It musta been unhuman strength what broke *that* blade. It was that good."

"Please, Master Bulldowne ... if you have the making of just one sword left in your arms ... would you make it for me?"

"Why, my Lady?" he asked. "What reason could you have?"

"It would be ... as a monument to my husband."

"Hmm." Old Bulldowne considered this for a moment, stroking his beard. "I could make you one that looked just like that sword for just a couple of eglons. Would that do?"

"Please ... I don't want one that just *looks* like that sword.... I would like you to remake that sword. Make it strong enough so that it could kill three more dragons. I have forty-seven eglons."

"A monument, eh?" He reached out and felt Hollie's arm, and she did not withdraw. "You'd never be able to swing a blade that heavy, Missy."

She looked at him steadily. "It is not my thought to swing that blade. It is for my husband's memory that I wish you to make it."

He regarded her with a solemn expression on his homely face. "Forged the steel seven times, I did. And young Roarke was fasting and praying the whole time I was working. If you really wanted to remake that blade ... you'd have to do your part, too. For the strength of that weapon weren't just in the metal."

Hollie said in a quiet voice, "I am not my husband. He was more noble than I am ... but I will try."

"Would you like to see the room where he prayed while I was poundin' metal? You can stay with us while I'm workin', if you like."

Hollie looked at him gratefully, a tired smile upon her face, as if the burden of her sorrow were momentarily lifted. "Yes, please."

ƴ

Will prayed, "I commit myself to Yer care, Iesuchristi God," as he strode directly to the sleeping dragon. Moving as if in a dream, he was amazed that he was allowed to get so close to the beast without waking it. Perhaps it was already dead? He advanced to the dragon's sinuous neck, lifted his sword over his head, and was one breath away from bringing the blade down, when the beast's eye fluttered open, and it raised its head from the earth.

Will brought the sword down on the serpent's neck, but it clanged off sideways, and was wrenched from his hands, landing in the square.

Will and the dragon regarded each other evenly, silently, for a moment. The spirit that had tormented Herm the Magician recognized Will, but it had not prepared a message for him in the dragon's puerile tongue. So, instead, the beast repeated the last song it had been taught to sing.

"AAAAAAAAAHHHHEEEEEEEE. COOOOMMMMMMMMM-MMMMMMMME."

"I ain't goin' to deliver yer message," Will heard himself saying. "I will kill ye today, or die myself, tryin'."

It didn't matter to the dragon whether Will delivered the message or not. It rose up from the earth, towering over the young knight. Will noticed the matted blood on the beast's chest, and saw that the left foreleg hung limp, useless. Blows had indeed been struck against the serpent ... maybe today was its day to die, after all.

Old Bulldowne said to his son, "Why don't you take a couple of days to rest with Geordie? Maybe you can make me that grandson you been promisin' me." (Geordie was Young Bulldowne's wife, and so far she had borne only daughters, four of them.)

"Got a job?" asked his son.

"Got a job."

Will walked coolly over to where his sword lay in the dirt, but he never took his eyes from the dragon, which snarled, a low threatening rumble. There was no trace of sport in the dragon's manner. The beast did not wish to play; it did not wish to work. It did not wish to eat; it did not even wish to kill. It wished to sleep, where alone it was free from the throbbing pain in its shoulder.

The beast stepped toward Will and lifted its rear leg to stomp on him and crush the life from him, but Will dodged the blow, deftly retrieving his sword as he darted away from the descending reptilian foot.

171

The dragon whipped its tail toward the knight, but it was too slow, and Will leaped over it. The beast stabbed its face toward him next, missing, teeth snapping noisily on air. Will slashed at the dragon's face as it passed, but again, the blow was glancing, and did the beast no harm.

Growling angrily now, the dragon stamped furiously around the square, trying to pin Will beneath one of its brawny rear legs. Will darted and dodged through the street, leaping the furrows that the dragon had dug. As he bounded over one of the ruts, though, he was shocked to see a tattered cloak that he recognized, its edges fluttering in the breeze, anchored to the ground by the remains of a man. The man's features were unrecognizable, but the tuft of white hair that still lifted from his shattered face revealed it to be Lord Roarke. Will involuntarily glanced back to look at his old friend, momentarily distracted from his pursuer.

The dragon's tail swept Will from his feet, and his sword landed about the length of his body away from him. Will rolled over onto his back, just in time to see the dragon's foot descending upon him, and he rolled again, the foot slamming to the ground just beside him.

He reached out and grabbed his sword, as the dragon once more lifted its leg to crush the life out of him. With not a second left to roll away this time, Will thrust his sword upward with the tip of his blade toward the sole of the monster's descending foot. The dragon stepped on the sword, which pierced its flesh and caused the beast to scream in rage and pain. It jerked its foot back skyward, away from the stabbing needle it had stepped on … but not before the weight of the blow had propelled the sword downward, breaking Will's arms, and causing the haft of the sword to be driven backward through his chest.

Sir Willum the Bold took two surprised, halting breaths … and breathed no more.

The dragon screeched and roared, its pain excruciating, and was filled with fury toward the unmoving man, who lay on his back staring at the sky. But the dragon did not step on him again.

Chapter Thirty-Two

King of the Dragon found Starlight grazing on some tufts of grass that poked through the snow on the southern edge of Solemon. He trotted up to the horse, and said, "Remember me? I'm yer friend, ain't I?" He patted the horse on the leg. "I wonder where Sir Willum's got to?"

He lifted his nose to the breeze, his nostrils twitching, but could detect no trace of his friend. Deciding then that must be Will had gone up the street into that town that was ahead of him, he jogged on in, though more cautiously. Must be the dragon was close by.

After some skulking, trepidatious moments stealing through the eerie, silent streets, the little gray kobold arrived in the center of town. And there it was—his second dragon. That was two more than Tilda and Vesta had ever seen, he reckoned. He licked his lips in anticipation of the feast that lay before him. The dragon was resting quietly with its eyes closed, just like the first one he had killed.

He wondered where Sir Willum was, and looked around the square, checking the empty wooden buildings to see if maybe he was hiding out someplace. All he saw was a sword sticking out of the ground, quite near where the dragon slept. Then he realized that the sword was standing erect with the tip of the blade pointing skyward, instead of the point being stuck down in the dirt, and he thought that was odd.

He hoped Sir Willum was all right, wherever he was. After he killed the dragon, he'd have to go looking for him. Maybe Will was sick. King of the Dragon hoped he had the kind of magic that healed sickness, as well as the kind he already knew about, the kind that killed dragons.

He hopped and pranced across the square, confident in his powers. He had not practiced any particular magic words, believing it was better just to let them come to him in their own way. He walked up to the dragon's face, stood right in front of it, and took a deep breath.

Then the King of the Dragon jumped up and down, bouncing in a circle, and shouted at the top of his voice, *"Hoogledy-poogledy-starnelly-blan! Wugga-wugga-wugga-wugga-blan! blan! blan!"*

He stopped jumping and stared wide-eyed at the dragon, holding his breath. Nothing happened. Nothing happened—just the way it was supposed to! King of the Dragon chuckled nervously to himself. Must be he had killed the dragon right out, just like the first time! He laughed a little louder, and then he danced for joy—triumphant, invincible.

Halting his exultant dance, he pulled a little knife out of its sheath on his belt, a little dagger that Esselte Smead had given to him. He thought he might use the knife to carve off a little morsel of dragon for dinner. Remembering his friend Smead, he wished he had a mug of mead to wash down the dragon, and unconsciously ran his tongue around his lips again. He looked forward to getting home to the comforts of Castle Thraill once more … after he found Sir Willum.

The dragon opened its eyes, and peered at the little gray being in front of its nose, annoyed that its rest was being disturbed again. The low rumble of a growl began to build in its belly. The King jumped, startled by the guttural vibrations.

He said quietly, *"Hoogledy—"*

Then he realized that the dragon was looking at him, and cried, "Eeep!" He turned to run, but the serpent stretched its jaws and snapped up the little kobold without even rising to its feet, and swallowed.

Old Bulldowne presented his workmanship to Hollie for her approval.

She was exhausted from prayer and weakened from fasting, but the skill with which the gleaming silver blade had been fashioned was obvious.

"It's ... magnificent," she said.

"I'll not make another." He placed the sword in her hands, and even though she had known it would be heavy, she still almost lost her grip on it.

"Oh!" Hollie gasped. "Forgive me!"

"No fear, my Lady. Leathersmith has made a sheath for it, and you should be able to carry it quite safely. And he's given you a purse, too, for holding bread and meat." He took the sword from her hands and laid it on a nearby table.

"Thank you ... but all I had was the forty-seven eglons I gave to you," she said with concern.

"I don't need that much gold, nor does my son. I gave five to Leathersmith, and five to Geordie, my son's wife, for the food she's preparin' for you. With the rest of the coins, well...."

He left the room for a moment, as Hollie wondered what he could mean. He reappeared in less than a minute.

"Here, my Lady. You might take this as a gift from the house of Bulldowne, and p'r'aps you'll recall us with kindness one day." He presented her with a round helmet of hammered metal, and she knew that it was the gold coins. "It's only gold, so it won't protect you from everything," Old

Bulldowne continued, "but it might save you from a nasty knock on the head, if God is smilin' on you that day."

She didn't know what else to say, so she softly replied, "Thank you."

Geordie came into the room then, bearing the leather purse heavily laden with bread and cold meat.

Hollie said, "Oh, my! That's so much food!"

"I only done what Old Bulldowne told me," Geordie said crossly.

"And you did right well, too," her father-in-law said with an approving grin.

"Thank you," Hollie said to the wild-haired man, gazing at him curiously. "But that's so much more food than I could ever eat on the way back to the castle."

"Well…. Well," he replied, "maybe you'll get a little hungry along the way."

She searched his eyes, wondering what it was that Old Bulldowne thought that he knew. "Thank you," she said, and stood on her toes and kissed him on both cheeks.

"God be with you, Missy," he grumbled, giving her a tender hug within his bear-like arms.

r

The dragon was dying. Her long centuries of malice were dwindling to a few fading days of agonized affliction. She had been weakened by the loss of blood due to Roarke's handiwork with his sword, but she probably would have recovered from those wounds. Then came the thunderous blow she had taken from the Defenders of Solemon, which had broken her left shoulder, and bruised her all through her chest and midsection. Again, she would have eventually recovered— mostly—though it was unlikely that she would have been able to ever use her left foreleg after her next century-long slumber.

Then came the wound that had been inflicted upon her by Sir Willum, or perhaps by herself when she was trying to step on Sir Willum. She had lost blood, and in her already weakened state, had grown listless and unable to rise.

But then came the worst blow of all. It was when she had eaten that little gray thing, which hadn't even been big enough to taste. But after she had swallowed and begun digesting the thing, she had started to feel violently ill. Her belly had distended, bloating to twice its normal size, straining against her skin, against her ribcage.

The massive beast lay on the ground, moaning, writhing in distress. She was dying. It *felt* like she was dying. It seemed that what King of the Dragon had conjectured to Sir Willum once, long ago—that he was poisonous to the dragon— may have in fact been the truth.

The demons inside her sensed that their grasp on her was slipping, slipping away, as the dragon wanted only to sleep, to die, wanted only to die. They knew that they were losing their hold on their last host, and were frustrated, angry, afraid. They willed the dragon to live. Live! Live!

And so the beast lingered on. It did not know why, but only lay on its side on the cold, rutted ground of Solemon, moaning in a soft growl, "Aaaaaheeee. Commmmmmme."

Chapter Thirty-Three

Hollie had never been to Solemon, and had never traveled anywhere by herself before, either. But she had discerned from listening to other conversations that, in order to find Solemon, what she needed to do was follow the King's Road from Lauren to where it crossed the river, and then just keep on heading east, straight east every day, and after a few days of steady riding, maybe a week, maybe a little longer ... she should be able to find the little town nestled in the foothills of the Senns.

She wore the gold helmet over her close-cropped hair, but kept it hidden underneath the hood of her cloak. She marveled at how well the helmet fitted her head, and wondered how Old Bulldowne had done it.

As she rode, she pondered the words of Mara Dannat's blessing to her at their parting, so many months ago. *Once has her heart been pierced, and twice. Her crown of gold is the glory of Hagenspan; and a mother of kings shall she be.* She had always figured she understood the part about her heart being pierced twice; she thought it referred to her first two children that had been taken from her. But now her heart had been pierced twice again ... she had lost Cedric ... she had lost Owan.

She had assumed that the crown of gold in the prophecy referred to her blonde hair, but now, she mused, that hair was gone ... but she really *did* wear a crown of gold—or at least a helmet of gold. What did it mean? Did it mean anything?

And then ... *a mother of kings*. She did not know how that could possibly come to pass. Though it seemed clear that Owan would at least be the Lord of Thraill someday; perhaps that's what it meant.

Maybe the prophecy just contained shadows, hints, generalizations. *Once has her heart been pierced, and twice.* Perhaps that just meant that her heart would be broken more than once—maybe many times. *Her crown of gold* ... maybe that meant her hair, *and* the golden helmet. *A mother of kings.* Well, a lord was pretty much the same as a king ... maybe that was as much as it meant. "I don't understand, Iesuchristi. But You must."

꜡

She had almost succumbed to despair during the night she had spent on the top of the mountain pass through the Sayls. The wind moaned and whined, and she imagined it was the voices of the spirits killed by the dragon, calling her, drawing her on toward her own doom. Or maybe it was the voice of the dragon itself ... but it meant the same thing.

It was so cold on the mountain that she barely slept at all, huddled behind a boulder, wrapped in her cloak. But she dared not ride on during the dark hours, for a misstep here would mean that she would never leave these cliffs.

The morning broke crisp and clean, though, and the sky was blue, bright blue, above the steely gray clouds which occasionally parted to let a golden beam of sunlight bless the mountaintop. As Hollie ate some of the food that had been provided for her by Old Bulldowne, she exhaled a silent prayer of thanksgiving.

꜡

"The road before me is dark ... perhaps it ends." She did not know whether she was praying or just speaking aloud, but the sound of a human voice—even her own—comforted her.

She had left the Sayls a day earlier, and was riding Joy across the plain. She felt sorry for her poor palfrey, who was suffering in this weather, with so little rest, with such poor fodder. She wished she had thought to take Justice, her husband's splendid war-horse, instead ... but she had not, and that was all there was to be said about that.

"We'll have to camp out here in the open tonight, dear," she said to the horse. "But we must be getting close. Close to something."

That night she drew her sword from its sheath, and laid the blade on her lap.

She placed her hands on the icy metal, and prayed, bargaining her life against the Almighty's favor. "Iesuchristi, my husband has been taken from me. My husband, that I loved. And my son, Owan, that You gave to me ... I have given him away. My husband, my son ... that I loved." She pursed her lips. "All I have left to offer is my life itself, the very breath that You gave me. And I do offer that, too." She was curious at how little emotion she felt, how detached she had become from the things that she formerly loved. "All I ask is that You will use me to accomplish the deliverance of this land, from the evil that haunts it. You may have my life, my soul, my breath, my strength. You may discard me at Your whim. But I beg You, please, Iesuchristi. Let me kill the dragon."

The sun was setting behind her back, a glorious display of orange and gold. But she ignored it, remained facing east. The beauties of this plane no longer belonged to her; she was bound to her doom. "Cedric believed that You are kind. I have no comment on that ... though Your kindness is severe indeed, if this rending of heart from body is Your doing ... this dying ... this suffering ... this hopelessness." She breathed evenly, steadily. "Cedric believed that our recompense would come when we joined You in Your land ... that we would be rewarded for our trials here, if we continued to trust You. Mara Dannat believed that, too. She called Your country a place where all our tears will be dried. I hope that it's true ... but I don't even ask for that. I will relinquish Your reward, if only you let me kill this dragon." She had no idea whether her prayers were heard, whether they were appropriate, whether they were blasphemous. But she knew, at least, that she was being honest. "Let me kill this dragon. For Owan. For Your people. For Hagenspan."

The absurdity of her—a mere woman—killing a dragon struck her suddenly as amusing, and she smiled. She sobered quickly, though, and said, "I know it's impossible for me to do this thing. But it must have been impossible for Cedric, too ... and yet he prevailed. He believed it to be a gift from You." She turned her face up toward the sky, all black and gray and midnight blue, without the glitter of star or glow of moon. "I beg You, Lord God Iesuchristi the Almighty One. Give me this gift too."

There was no answer. No light appeared in the sky, no holy voice whispered comforting words in her ear. There was only the mournful moan of the wind, its desolate spectral sigh sounding a sorrowful lament as the phantom spirits wove around her, caressing her face, her throat, calling silently, *Hollie ... come.*

Chapter Thirty-Four

Porcatie saw the rider coming from the west, and shook his head sadly. Another knight, on his way to deliver himself to the jaws of the dragon. This one, perhaps, Porcatie would spare the indignity of failing to kill the beast ... this one he would just kill himself.

He stepped out from the brush at the northern border of the forest, and shouted a greeting. "Hallo, Sir Knight!" He ran toward the rider, stumbling and cursing.

Hollie saw the man coming toward her, and recognized him immediately. She couldn't remember his name (if she had ever known it), and he was filthy and much thinner than when she had last seen him, but there was no mistaking it—this man had been one of her ... *patrons* ... when she had worked for Kenndt back in Ruric's Keep. She suddenly felt unclean, defiled. She thought that perhaps she should put her heels to Joy, and ride on past him. But then she realized that he must be desperate and alone. Perhaps she could help him. Perhaps Iesuchristi had appointed this meeting. And, if not ... she had her sword.

"Sir Knight," Porcatie gasped, reaching out his hand to grab the horse's bridle. He looked up at the rider, and felt a jolt of surprise. "You're a woman!"

He looked more closely. "Why ... you're Kenndt's Hollie!"

"I am not," Hollie replied stiffly. "I am Lady Hollie Roarke, wife of Sir Cedric Roarke, Lord of Thraill and Blythecairne."

"Of course, of course," Porcatie apologized. "But you *used* to be Kenndt's Hollie. Do you, ah ... do you remember me?"

185

She stared icily off into the distance for a moment before she answered. "I know that we have met, but I have forgotten your name."

"That's all right, my Lady, it's of no consequence. Though if you're interested, it's Porcatie."

"Yes. Thank you."

"Let me lead you to camp, where you can rest for a bit before you go on your way. I have food and water, and I can build a fire."

"Very well."

ɼ

When Hollie arrived at Porcatie's camp, she was surprised to find that he had two horses, and wondered why he was hiding here in the forest instead of going home to Ruric's Keep. Then she recognized that one of the animals was Willum's Starlight.

"That horse," she said to Porcatie, "belongs to Sir Willum of Blythecairne."

"Did," he replied simply.

"What do you mean?" Hollie asked, though she thought she probably understood.

"Sir Willum went riding off to Solemon about a week ago. Maybe it was a little more, now. Anyway, he didn't come back, and a couple of days later, his horse was heading back to the west, so I caught him."

"Oh." Hollie figured that she should be sad, but she had roamed far beyond the place where she was able to accommodate any more sorrow.

She no longer mourned for Cedric or for Owan, and could not begin to mourn for Will, either, poor Will. Maybe later ... if there *was* a later.

ɼ

Porcatie had built a large fire, and even though it was quite warm in the camp, Hollie had not removed her hood. She felt that it was wisest for her to keep her features as hidden as possible from Porcatie's searching eyes.

They had eaten until they were full, but Porcatie still possessed an obvious hunger. He leered at Hollie openly, recalling their earlier encounters with a fondly rekindled lust. He feigned courtesy, but became more and more familiar with her as the evening progressed.

"Warm?" he asked.

"Yes," Hollie replied without inflection.

"Well, then ... why don't you just shinny off them pants, and we'll have a little taste of something."

"Excuse me?" she said incredulously.

"You heard me right. It ain't like I never been there before."

Hollie blanched, furious. She knew that her situation was perilous, and breathed a quick prayer. This could not be!

"I am a married woman," she said severely.

"Your husband's dead. Sorry about that, but it's so."

"I am on my way to do battle with the dragon!"

"All the more reason. I wasn't going to let you go and get killed by the dragon anyway, but even if I did, why not give me four minutes of pleasure before you went?"

Her voice rose. "I am holy to the Lord Iesuchristi!" she said, feeling for her sword.

"He won't care," Porcatie said rudely. "Ask him to stop me, and see if he does."

"If you touch me, I will kill you myself," she said, and drew the blade that Old Bulldowne had forged for her.

Porcatie laughed. "I think I'll go ahead and touch you anyway, and then let you kill me." He laughed again, mocking her. "I don't expect you'd really prick me with that thing anyway ... though it is a pretty blade." He grinned at her. "There might be blood."

At that, he picked up a flaming bough from the fire and used it to swat Hollie's sword away. She lost her grip on the haft, and it fell to the ground.

"Thought so," Porcatie said.

He stretched his arm out and grabbed her hood, yanking it from her head. She reached up and put her hands on her golden helmet, clutching it tightly to her skull.

"What happened to your hair?" asked Porcatie, intrigued. Not waiting for a response, he pulled Hollie close to him and tried to force a kiss from her.

Hollie jerked her helmet off and brought it down on the top of Porcatie's head with both hands.

"Ouch! Damn you!" Porcatie cursed, and drew back his fist to deal her a clout on the jaw. Before he could strike, though, she gave him another ringing knock in the head with the helmet. He loosed his grip on her cloak, and she wrenched free.

Staggering drunkenly, Porcatie reached for her again, and she swung with the helmet one more time, catching him on the left temple. Porcatie dropped to the ground like a sack of rocks and did not stir.

Breathlessly, she replaced the helmet upon her head and retrieved her sword. Not waiting to see whether he was dead or alive, she climbed upon Joy and rode briskly out of the woods, leaving Porcatie lying on the dirt next to the fire.

ſ

After the oppressive heat of the campfire, coupled with the intensity of her exertions in avoiding her attacker, Hollie was very, very cold that night.

If she had contained tears, she would have shed them, but apparently she had none. What she had was sweat, which froze against her skin, causing her to shudder and tremble.

She huddled in a shivering mound upon the earth, tormented by the wind, tormented by memory of Porcatie's repulsive attitude. She pulled her cloak about her more tightly, trying to deny the wind any point of access ... but she could not deny the entrance of Porcatie's mocking words into her mind.

She chastised herself that she had not been able to defend herself with the sword. What on earth was she going to do against the dragon? Desperately, she prayed for a miracle.

Chapter Thirty-Five

Esselte Smead sat at his desk, listlessly staring at a small stack of papers but not reading the words written upon them.

He wondered why Hollie had left, why she had felt it necessary to steal away under the cover of darkness, why she had had to assault the guard as she departed. Not much of a guard, Baniff, according to his reports, but still ... why had Hollie crept up behind him and smashed him on the side of the face without so much as a warning?

It was true that she had been acting a little, well, unbalanced, ever since Cedric had been reported dead. How else could one explain the fact that she had left without taking her baby? A *mother*, leaving her baby ... it was nearly unthinkable.

Smead feared that he had driven her away. *You will always be my Lady, in whatever realm you wish to be.* What an idiot he had been. He ducked his head as if he had just received a blow.

His gaze strayed from the stack of papers to the empty tankard from which King of the Dragon used to drink his draughts of watered-down mead. He missed the little kobold, more than he thought possible. He hoped the little fellow was all right.

ſ

Ronica Tenet clucked softly to the baby boy Owan, her brother's son, making doting, nonsensical noises. She had never had a little boy of her own, not before ... but now she did.

Owan burbled and cooed back at her, smiling his wide toothless grin. He grabbed her finger and held on tightly.

Ronica gushed, "Oh, aren't you a strong little man? Just like your daddy! I'll tell you all about him, when you're big enough to understand."

She never spoke to the little boy about his mother. Ronica viewed Hollie as an unfortunate parenthetical episode in her brother's life— necessary only to produce this charming little boy, the future Lord of Thraill. Ronica's nephew.

Ronica's son.

ʃ

Captain Hess Boole entered the door of Bulldowne's smithy, politely asking if anyone there had recently seen the Lady Hollie, who was Lord Cedric Roarke's widow.

Young Bulldowne wiped his arms with his cloth, and said, "Yes, she was here some time back. My wife made a meal for her."

Boole exclaimed, "At last! We feared she had vanished completely from the borders of Haioland! Where is she now?"

"Oh, she's been gone for days. Longer."

Testily, Boole asked, "Well, which way did she go?"

Young Bulldowne replied, "We didn't watch her leave. But she *said* she was heading back to Castle Thraill."

ʳ

Haldamar stood at the door to Paipaerria's bedroom, looking in with concern at his daughter. "Couldn't you at least try to eat something?"

"I will … later. I'm not really hungry, Daddy."

"All right," he said. "I just hate seeing you mourn like this."

She turned her sorrowful eyes toward her father and said, "Somebody needs to mourn."

Haldamar was silent for a moment before he softly said, "We don't even know for certain that he's dead."

Piper gave her father a faint, indulgent wisp of a smile, but there was no mirth in her eyes. "All right, Daddy."

ʳ

Keet, the steward of Blythecairne, often wondered about his son, and mentioned him to God every morning in his prayers. He wondered what Will had seen, what adventures he had had, whether he had found friendship, whether he had found love?

He hoped that somehow his boy had not gone off to battle the dragon, hoped against hope that it was so. But he also reckoned that if the young men of Hagenspan were called from every quarter of the country— some had even gone out from Blythecairne—then Will must have heard the call too. And he lived with Lord Roarke, for mercy's sake—how would *he* have not been called to action?

So Keet knew that there was a very real possibility that he would never see his son again. He had known that before he sent him forth from his home to visit the west. But this, of course, was different.

The steward of Blythecairne had received sketchy reports from Solemon. The most notable detail, though, was the sad fact that none of the young men who went to do battle directly with the dragon of Beale's Keep ever made another report again. The only news that had been delivered to the castle was from traveling merchants and bands of entertainers, never from the men who had actually been sent to fight. So everything that Keet knew was either rumor, or conjecture, or lie.

Still, he clung to the faint hope that his good little Will would come home again someday and fill his arms with a man's strong embrace, and he mentioned him to God every morning in his prayers.

Chapter Thirty-Six

The wind whistled down the street that led to the center of Solemon, an icy blast that chilled Hollie's very bones. Her teeth clattered together, her arms shook, and her hands were numb, her fingers unfeeling nubs. It felt as if the golden helmet were frozen to her skull. Snow blew into her face, melting against her unblinking eyes.

She had no passion to kill the dragon. She felt no anger against the beast, not any more. Her sunken orbs stared dully up the street toward her destination ... her destiny. She didn't even know how she knew that the dragon was ahead of her in the square. All that drove her on was the knowledge that something lay before her which had to be done, which absolutely *must* be done, and then, after that ... rest. After that, she could rest.

She arrived in the square, saw the bloated dragon lying on its side, and for one terrified instant thought that it had already expired. *Oh, no,* she thought. *If the dragon is already dead ... then who is left to kill* me? Then she saw it draw a rasping breath, and was relieved.

She climbed down off her exhausted horse, and kissed it on the side of its face. *Goodbye, Joy.* Then she walked slowly toward the dragon, which rolled over onto its belly and watched her approach.

Hollie noted Cedric lying on the ground, crushed. Next to him was Will, apparently affixed to the earth by his own bloodstained sword. They looked so peaceful. She was coming to join them.

The dragon opened its mouth and groaned, "Aaaaaaaaaaheee-eeeeeeeee."

She looked at the huge serpent, feeling no awe, feeling only a vague sense of revulsion. She whispered, "Let's be done with this."

The dragon heaved itself to its feet, staggering, weaving, lurching. Hollie slowly drew her sword from its sheath. *God ... it was so heavy.*

With an effort, she brought the blade up in front her face, pointing it at the serpent's snout. The dragon growled, remembering faintly that it hated, hated, hated.

Bending its teetering head down toward Hollie, the serpent opened its mouth to bite. From somewhere inside the beast, one tiny voice shouted out that this was the morsel it had been waiting for ... this was the thing which had been forestalling the serpent's long-coveted slumber.

Hollie saw the dragon's maw stretched wide to receive her, saw the teeth like rows of daggers descending to piece her flesh. She felt a moment of panic. *I am too small!*

Suddenly, it was as if a voice inside Hollie's head commanded her: *Turn!* She turned and began to run away from the dragon, but she was too slow. The serpent's mouth covered her, and all the brightness of the world turned to shadow. *Jump!* Hollie leaped, as well as she could, straight up into the air, and the daggerlike trap of the dragon's teeth snapped shut all around her.

She felt herself lifted into the air, seemingly—she became dizzy with vertigo, even as she was being suffocated by the cloying viscidity of the serpent's saliva. But the dragon's teeth had not pierced her. She realized that she was lying on her back on the dragon's tongue, and that she still held her sword above her face; in fact, the flat of the blade was being pressed against her own cheek.

The dragon opened its mouth to try to get a better purchase on its prize, and Hollie was momentarily freed from the claustrophobic press of her slithering confinement. She saw the roof of the dragon's mouth looming above her as light streamed in, and quickly pushed the point of the sword upward into the serpent's soft upper palate.

The dragon bit down again, once again missing Hollie's limbs with its teeth. But as the serpent's mouth clamped shut, the blade of the sword—the steel that had been forged seven times and strengthened with prayer and fasting—the sword fashioned like the sword of Roarke the Dragon-Killer, which Herm the Magician had broken—the sword of Hollie Roarke, the Dragon-Killer's widow—*that* sword was forced through the top of the dragon's mouth, pushing its way deep into the dragon's brain. And the hateful fire that had burned against the people of Hagenspan for two violent centuries was extinguished.

The dragon toppled over onto its face with a shattering concussion. And in the square of Solemon, all was still ... all except the piteous whine of the wind.

Chapter Thirty-Seven

Padallor Clay, the Last Defender of Solemon, was starving. It no longer mattered whether the dragon was going to kill him or not; he was going to die. It was time for him to rouse himself from his place of refuge and add his last blow to the battle.

When Paddy had run from the dragon after the disaster with the crossbow, he had thought only to return to Bedford's Tap, but with the dragon roaring after him up the street and gaining on him with every step, he had turned to the side, dived in amongst some wreckage, and to his immense good fortune had found himself tumbling into the dugout basement of a ruined house. He had lain silently on the earthen floor of the cellar, watching the dusty beams of light filter down through the ruins, waiting until there was no trace of noise from outside before he dared to move so much as a finger.

When he had explored his dark haven, he had found to his amazement some strips of dried meat that had been left behind, forgotten in some family's terrified exodus from their home, left behind to nourish the Last Defender of Solemon. He had lived off that meat for more than two weeks, eating tiny rations each day, just enough to keep him from utter starvation.

Sometimes he heard the dragon stomp through the streets, muttering, growling. Maybe the damnable beast was looking for *him*. He stayed under the ground, growing pale and weak … but not dead. Once or twice he heard the soft clop of a horse heading for the center of town, realized another knight was going to feed himself to the dragon, and said a prayer for his soul. He had peeked out at one of them once, watching him as he rode toward the town square, and then a few moments later he had seen the knight's horse heading back out of town. He had not seen the knight again.

Paddy's food supply had finally been exhausted two days past. He had heard once somewhere that a man could only live three days without food. He didn't know if that was the truth or not, but he knew he was getting weaker every day anyway. If he was ever going to strike one last blow against the dragon, it would have to be now, or it would never happen.

He gathered his weapons—a sword that had belonged to one of the boys from Blythecairne, and the bow that he had carried ever since he had left Katarin. How long ago had that been? No matter … he did not expect to see the comfortable streets of his hometown again. He trudged toward the square—a place he knew far too well. His legs were feeble from hunger and inactivity, and he was panting before he reached his destination.

To his surprise, he found a horse waiting patiently at the end of the street just before it opened up into the square. A nice-looking horse, too, if a bit poorly used. There were saddlebags on its flanks; maybe there was even food! He would check, if somehow he survived the day. But he did not want to be seduced by the prospect of food—not now. If he were to go slinking back into hiding, what would be the point? To slowly starve himself to death again, and then come right back to this same place anyway?

Turning his attention to the square, he strode forward and saw his old enemy lying in the dirt, apparently asleep. Notching an arrow to his bowstring, he took another step forward, and paused to look more closely.

The dragon's eye was open. It knew he was there! But … no … it was just staring off into space, its gaze vacant, void of any thought. Could it be …that the damned thing was already *dead*?

He stepped cautiously toward the beast, then took another step, and another. The dragon was dead. The dragon was dead! He observed bitterly that that should have been happy news ... but he felt nothing but anger. Disgust. Impotence. Determined that, at last, he would strike his blow against the damned, God*damned* creature anyway, Paddy stepped up to where the dragon stared emptily back at him. He drew his bow. "This is for Billy Spreg," he said, and let the shaft fly, piercing the beast's eye and lodging in its head.

Feeling scant satisfaction, Paddy walked around to the other side of the dragon's face, fitted another arrow to his bow, said, "And this one's for me." After firing the arrow into the dead beast's eye, he turned away in frustrated loathing, thinking that he should probably offer some kind of apology to God for his foul attitude. After all, the dragon was dead, which was supposedly the very thing he had been praying for. He felt like growling himself.

From behind him, he heard a faint moan coming from the dragon's mouth. His heart leaped in his chest, pounding audibly, throbbing painfully. It *wasn't* dead!

The moan passed through the dragon's lips again ... and Paddy realized that it wasn't the serpent's voice at all—somebody was *in* there!

"Hang on!" he cried. "I'll get you out!"

Taking his sword, he pried open the dragon's mouth a bit, and saw boots. Unable to work the beast's jaw open any further, he said again, "Hang on," and wedged stones between the dragon's teeth to keep the mouth from snapping shut.

"That's the best I can do," Paddy said breathlessly. "I'm sorry, but I'm goin' to hafta drag you across the dragon's teeth. I hope it don't hurt too bad."

He reached in and grabbed the person's ankles, and started tugging. After a fatiguing struggle to work the warrior out of the dragon's mouth while causing that one to suffer as little damage as possible, Paddy finally saw the face of the deliverer of Hagenspan—saw with amazement that it was a woman. Her face even looked vaguely familiar, but something was wrong.

Then he realized that what was wrong was that her hair was mostly gone— and he recognized her with a start. It was the Lady Hollie, the great beauty of the land, about whom songs were sung. It was the gentle, laughing Lady Hollie, who had let Paddy shake her hand, so long ago in Castle Blythecairne. Hollie, whose husband, the Lord Roarke, Paddy had seen die beneath the dragon's heel, after making his last valiant stand.

It was Hollie.

She looked up into Paddy's eyes, and did not—or could not—speak. Paddy could not tell if she was conscious or unconscious, and his own eyes blurred with tears.

"It's all right, Lady Hollie. I'll take care of you now." His last vestiges of composure dissolved, and he wept, sobbing jaggedly … all of the frustration, bitterness, and bereavement of the past year finally released in an excruciating, cleansing torrent of tears.

Chapter Thirty-Eight

At the southernmost reaches of the fields of Blythecairne, Spence walked his pony in a little circuit, performing his regular turn of guard duty. Because Spence had been approved to go and spend time with the Amendicarii the following spring, he was no longer required to take a turn at the far reaches, but he willingly volunteered anyway.

Spence considered it to be a great honor to be committed to learning about God, and he took pleasure in these lonely times of sentry duty, since they afforded him ample time for prayer and contemplation. He even took some pleasure in physical discomfort, for he felt it offered him a greater opportunity for learning humility.

He was feeling very humble today, for it was a day of blustery, drifting snow, and Spence had forgotten to wear gloves. He kept his hands tucked into the folds of his mantle as well as he could, but he was still rather cold and miserable. He was fairly certain the castle was safe, for no one would be about on a day like this, not even itinerant merchants ... just the sentries.

So Spence was quite surprised when he saw, walking through the blowing snow, a figure leading a horse, upon which rode another person. Raising his horn to his lips, he sounded a long, bittersweet tone, and then urged his pony up to the pair of unfortunate travelers.

The tattered, emaciated man who led the horse stopped and waited for Spence to draw near. "We're friends," he called.

"How can I help ye, friends?" Spence asked uneasily.

"The Lady of Blythecairne has returned," Paddy said.

ſ

Around the great wooden table in the hall of Meadling sat Lirey, Keet, the brigadiers, and Padallor Clay, who had been telling them the sad story of Solemon and the dragon. Keet was weeping openly, for he now knew the fate of his beloved son, whom Paddy had buried beneath the dirt of Solemon next to Lord Roarke.

Lirey said, "The rest o' the boys we sent out from here ... did they serve ye proud?"

Paddy replied sincerely, "I was only blessed enough to know Tinker, but he was just about as fine's a boy as I spent a day with. We was like right hands to each other, there, for a little while. If he was any clue of the kind of boy you sent forth from Blythecairne, well, they were the best."

Lirey nodded sadly. "Then ... ye were the only one that lived? Out of *every*body?"

"So far's I know. Lady Hollie, of course."

"And Hollie's the one? The one what kilt the dragon?"

Paddy choked out, "As best as I can tell ... Lord Roarke did it some damage, and then me and the boys dealt it a cruel blow." He looked apologetically at Keet. "I expect your Sir Willum laid a few stripes on it, too. But it was Hollie that did it in."

"Who all knows that the dragon's dead?" Lirey asked.

"Just you folks, I believe," Paddy guessed.

Lirey addressed Yancey Wain. "Get some messengers ready. We'll need a pair t' go t' Ruric's Keep t' tell the king. And a pair fer Castle Thraill, t' tell 'em that Lady Hollie's still alive, but that she'll be winterin' with us here, an' recoverin' from her ails."

Lirey looked at Paddy Clay. "Ye've done us a service, bringin' our Lady home t' us. An' that's not t' mention the service ye done fer the king, fightin' fer so long against the dragon. Now ... what can Blythecairne do fer ye?"

"Thank you kindly, Captain. I just long to go home to see my own Sarie again, if she'll still have me. I had to cross the road to Katarin to bring Lady Hollie here, you know, and ... darned if I didn't want to turn up that road for home." He brushed a tear from his cheek. "Can you maybe loan me a horse?"

"Aye," Lirey said soberly, "it'd be our honor t' help ye get home t' yer wife."

The men sat around the table in grim silence for a moment, staring at their hands. Lirey's chest heaved with a mighty sigh. "Ye know ... none of us had any right t' ever expect t' see Lord Roarke in this life again, an' maybe not Will neither. But—but—" He was unable to continue his thought.

Keet said in a broken voice, "I take yer meanin'. Th' world's a poorer place today without 'em."

"Aye. That's it."

ŗ

Hollie lay in a bed, covered with quilts, and Maryan and Thalia sat with her. She had been back in Blythecairne for a week, and had not spoken to them yet, though she allowed them to minister to her needs, feed her broth, stroke her brow. She smiled at them faintly, feeling that she knew who they were—that they were friends—and confident that she would remember in time.

She opened her mouth and made a dry sound. She swallowed painfully, moistening her throat, and tried again. "Where ... is Owan?"

Maryan and Thalia looked at each other helplessly, and Maryan apologized, "We don't know who Owan is, Hollie."

Hollie looked confused, as if she were not really sure who Owan was, either. Then she said in a pitiful voice, "Cedric is dead." Tears came to her eyes.

Maryan gathered her in her arms, and said, "I know, sweetheart. I'm so sorry."

Hollie let her friend hold her, stroke her, pet her, and she rested her head against Maryan's soft brown hair. She whispered, "I killed the dragon."

Chapter Thirty-Nine

Paddy Clay looked longingly at the door of The Cold Fish as he rode past on his borrowed horse. He hoped the boys would still remember him, and maybe buy him a round, seeing as how he didn't have any money of his own. He wished he had thought to ask Captain Lirey for some, back when Lirey had asked what Blythecairne could do for him. They probably could have spared him a ruric or two. Well, no matter now—he had to go and beg Sarie to take him back, and it wouldn't help for him to come to her with liquor on his breath.

He tried to calculate how long he had been gone, and judging from the changing of the seasons, he figured it might have been about half a year. That wasn't too long, he supposed, not for fighting a dragon. He hoped Sarie felt the same.

He turned down the alley that led to the little house that he had shared with his wife. The features of the alley appeared comfortably familiar to him—homey. He noticed that Mulgrew had still not fixed his fence, and saw that Missus Fenter's cats were still lying in a crowded pile of fur outside her door, just as they had done since Paddy was a little boy. He saw a tangle of fishing poles leaning against the wall of Purley's, and suddenly wanted to go fishing so bad he could taste it.

Almost before he had realized it was happening, he was turning aside into his own dooryard ... Sarie's, he meant. He saw the wash hanging on the line, noticed some colored bits of clothing he didn't recognize, and suddenly his sense of familiarity, of coming home, was lost.

Thinking that perhaps what he really needed, after all, was to head back to The Fish for a pint on credit, he started to turn the horse back up the alley in the other direction. Before he got the horse properly circled around, though, he heard her voice.

"Padallor Clay."

"Hello, Sar'." Paddy's heart thumped rapidly as he turned to look at her. "Are you glad to see me?"

"That's a nice horse," she said noncommittally. "I don't know if I'm glad to see you or not."

"It ain't mine," Paddy said uneasily. "It's borrowed."

She stood with her arms crossed, blocking the doorway to their kitchen. Paddy thought she looked a little tired, and said so.

"Well, you would be too, if you had to...." Her voice trailed off. "Are you going to get down?"

"If it ain't too much trouble," Paddy said hesitantly.

"Not for me," Sarie consented.

"Is it all right if I come in?"

"I don't know," Sarie said reluctantly. "What are you here for?"

"Well, I, ah ... we're married, Sar'."

"That didn't stop you from runnin' off to fight a dragon when I didn't want you to do no such thing."

Paddy wore a pained expression upon his honest face. "I don't know what to say. I thought it was the right thing to do ... when I done it."

"Is that all you have to say to me, Paddy Clay?" she demanded softly.

"Well ... no, I guess." He wondered what words would convince her how earnestly he wanted to repent. "I'll beg if you want me to, Sar'. I'll get down on my knees and beg—God's my witness. There ain't nothin' in the world I want more than to just live with you, quiet and simple, for all the rest of our days."

"That's right," she said. "You'd better say that, if you mean it." She hesitated. "But it ain't so simple as that, Paddy. You've been gone quite a long spell, and ... well ... I've got another man in my life now, kind of."

"No, Sar' ... don't let it be," Paddy said, his voice pale and wavering. He felt like he'd just been kicked in the stomach, like his last reason for living was fading like a vapor.

Sarie saw his pain, and felt a pang of remorse. "You've been gone an awful long time."

"But you said ... you said—" Paddy choked. He turned and started to climb back up onto the horse, so she wouldn't see him break down.

"What did I say, Paddy?"

"I'm sorry, Sar'. I should be goin'."

"What did I say?"

He looked at her for a long, aching moment. "You said you'd always keep the door open for me." He fought to control the muscles of his face. "I can't tell you how many times I thought o' them words over the weeks."

She looked at him steadily, thinking, remembering. "I did say that, didn't I?" She unfolded her arms, and kicked open the door without looking. "You might as well come in."

"But—"

"But what?"

209

"What about *him*?" The words tasted like bile in his mouth. "The other man?"

"Well, you'll just have to get used to him, I guess, like I did." She stood at the door waiting for him to get down from the saddle. "Come on."

Confused, Paddy mutely obeyed, walking slowly toward his door, his house, his wife. Before he got to the wooden landing where she waited for him, though, she presented her terms.

"Paddy, if I let you back into my life again, you got to promise me that there won't be no more adventuring, no more running off to God only knows where. If you're going to be my husband, then that's what I want you to be. You got to settle down and be that."

"I will."

"I mean it, Paddy."

"I promise I will."

She looked at him for a moment longer, as he waited, unsure of whether he was being allowed to proceed. "Then come on up here, and let me give you a squeeze," she said softly, and tears sprung to her eyes. "I surely have missed you."

Paddy stepped up onto the little porch and took her into his arms. He was finally overcome with emotion, and sobbed against her neck for some time. She patted his shoulders, waiting patiently for him to regain control.

When at last he was able to speak, he said brokenly, "You feel so good in my arms." He exhaled, a long, jagged sigh. "I didn't think ... I didn't think I'd ever feel you there again."

Sarie smiled tenderly and said, "Come on inside, Paddy Clay." She led him by the hand into the kitchen. After hesitating just a moment, she said, "Well ... I guess you'd better meet him now."

"He's here?"

"In the bedroom."

Paddy was still buffeted by confusion, so he didn't know whether to be furious, or what. But Sarie tugged his hand, and he followed his wife into their bedroom, wondering what on earth was going to happen next.

Lying in the center of the bed, bundled in a cloth, was a tiny baby, not more than two weeks old. Sarie sat on the edge of the bed, reached out and gathered him up into her arms.

"Come, look, Paddy. Come and meet your baby boy."

With a face full of wonderment, Paddy Clay knelt down next to his wife and stared in awe at the tiny infant. "I don't ... understand," he said. "How could it be mine? I ... been gone."

"Well, you ain't been gone that long!" she said in mock exasperation. "He was already in the oven when you left."

Paddy peered down at the tiny face, the tiny fingers. "You mean, he's mine?" She nodded. "My son?" She nodded again, smiling.

"What's his name?"

Sarie said apologetically, "I hope you don't mind ... but I've been calling him Billy."

Paddy shook his head happily. "No, that's fine. That's ... fine!"

He reached out with a finger and softly touched his son's tiny hand.

"Hello, little Bill," he whispered. "It's me, your Dad. I been away," he explained. "I'll tell you all about it one day."

Chapter Forty

The following spring, Esselte Smead sent Hess Boole and a small company of guards from Castle Thraill to Blythecairne, to fetch the Lady Hollie and bring her home. If the truth were to be known, though, Hollie would have preferred to live out her days at Blythecairne instead ... if it had not been for her son, Owan.

Hollie had reclaimed her reason, her judgment—reclaimed her dignity— during the snow-covered months of her recovery, surrounded by the warmth of her friends. And she had mourned. They all had mourned at Blythecairne, marking the passing of Lord Roarke and their Sir Willum the Bold, whom they had loved. Hollie, though, mourned all the more for the loss of her baby boy, who was still alive in the western lands, but beyond the reach of her arms.

Ronica Tenet had not been pleased to hear that her sister-in-law still lived, though she was forced to feign admiration and delight and joy and relief. After all, Hollie had killed the dragon and delivered Hagenspan. Smead and Haldamar had made it pointedly clear that she was to give Owan back to his mother when Hollie arrived at Castle Thraill. Ronica had to comply, though secretly she felt once again as if she had been cheated out of the inheritance that was due her.

ʃ

King Ruric had received the report that Lady Hollie, the widow of Roarke the Dragon-Killer, had been the one who had delivered Hagenspan from the serpent. He had also heard that Hollie had not struck the only blow—just the final one. The report he received stated that Sir Roarke had done damage, Sir Willum had probably done damage, and that the king's crossbow had struck a crucial, decisive blow—the one that probably was ultimately responsible for the dragon's death.

When he was reminded of the promise he had made when commissioning his knights, that "whoever kills this last dragon shall be rewarded with the Lordship of Beale's Keep, and every acre of County Temter that lies between the Sayls and the Senns," he decided sensibly to change his mind.

"Since it was the weapon of your own design that undoubtedly killed the beast, you should keep the acreage between the Sayls and the Senns as an everlasting heritage to your own wisdom," said the king's most trusted advisor, Herm. "Sir Roarke and Sir Willum are dead, so no concession needs be made to them."

"And how shall we reward the Lady Hollie?" the king wondered.

"You shall give her Beale's Keep," Herm recommended. "A prize worth far more than she ever could have dreamed of, back when she lived here in your city."

"Beale's Keep," King Ruric mused thoughtfully. "It is probably in ruins."

"Perhaps."

"Here is what we shall do," the king decided. "We shall give the Lady Hollie the castle of Beale's Keep, plus all of the land she can traverse in one day's walking, to the north, to the south, to the east, and to the west. That way she will have fields for her providing."

"How wise," Herm purred. "How generous of you, O King."

Ɍ

Sir Herbert rode doubtfully through the streets of Katarin, soliciting directions from tattered and gawking townspeople, who finally pointed him down the alley toward where the Clays lived, Paddy and Sarie and Billy. Sir Herbert was a very young knight, beardless and slender, and this was his first mission on behalf of King Ruric. Since so many of the king's knights had not returned from their quest to deliver Solemon, there were few left to attend to his business; that was why young Sir Herbert rode alone.

After mistakenly making a fruitless stop at Purley's next door, Sir Herbert finally arrived in Paddy's dooryard. He debated calling out his arrival from the back of his horse, then decided to dismount and knock at the door.

"Who's there?" a female voice demanded.

"I, ah—it's, ah," Sir Herbert replied.

The door opened, and a gentle-looking man stood there, smiling apologetically. "You'll have to forgive my wife," he said. "She's a bit suspicious of strangers."

"Are you Padallor Clay?" Sir Herbert asked.

"That I am."

"I have a message for you from King Ruric himself."

"Is that so?" Paddy asked, impressed. "I wouldn't have thought the king knew who I was."

"Reports of your endurance in the war against the dragon have reached his ear. He knows much," Sir Herbert said primly. "May I read his message to you?"

215

"Certainly," Paddy replied. "Why don't you come in, so Sarie can hear it too?"

"Very well."

They stepped into the little kitchen. "Sarie, this is—I'm sorry, I forgot to get your name."

"I am Sir Herbert, my lady, and I bring word from the king."

"King Ruric?"

"Of course."

"Oh, my," Sarie said anxiously. "Paddy, what's it mean?"

"I guess we'll know after Sir Herbert reads his message," Paddy said with a relaxed, comfortable smile. He had survived half a year fighting with the dragon, and Sir Herbert didn't look to be quite so ferocious as that.

"May I?" the young knight asked.

"Please."

Sir Herbert produced a small scroll, unrolled it, and began to read:

Ruric the Third, King of Hagenspan, called Serpent's-Bane, to our Most Faithful Subject Padelore Clay:

With the number of Knights having been Greatly Diminished in the course of their failure to subdue that beast known as The Dragon, and since you have not only survived The Battle but were also there to witness Its Demise, it is Our Most Earnest Desire that you, Padelore Clay, accept a Commission as Knight Errant of the Northren Relm of Hagenspan and be henseforth known as Sir Padelore the Stedfast.

Report to us Forthwith at The Royal Castle in Ruric's Keep, and we shall be both Obliged and Honored to present you with Our Commission.

Signed by our own hand,

Ruric Serpent's-Bane

Sarie laid a trembling hand on Paddy's arm, torn by conflicting emotions. She was terribly afraid of losing her husband to another adventure … but also very proud of him. A knight! Who ever would have dreamed?

"Will you then accompany me back to Ruric's Keep?" Sir Herbert asked.

"Hmm," pondered Padallor Clay. "I believe I will … respectfully decline."

"What?" asked a surprised Sir Herbert.

"What?" exclaimed a startled Sarie Clay.

"I promised my wife that I wouldn't go off doin' no more exploits— that I'd stay home and take care of her and little Bill," Paddy said reasonably. "You can thank the king for me most kindly, but I guess I don't need to be a knight."

"I'm not sure you can … refuse," said Sir Herbert with consternation.

"Well, you go and find out, and if I can't, you can come back and get me," Paddy said, directing the young knight back to his horse.

"But—"

"Thank the king for me. Tell him he's always welcome here, to stop and pay a visit."

217

Looking confused, Sir Herbert mounted his horse.

Paddy had a thought, and said, "Say ... you don't suppose I could have that letter, do you?"

The knight handed him the scroll. "I ... believe so."

"Thanks much. It might make somethin' interestin' to show little Bill someday."

The knight slapped the reins of his horse and left the dooryard, but turned at the gate and looked back at Paddy, who waved at him with a small smile. Sir Herbert raised a hand, saluting the Last Defender of Solemon, and departed back up the alley.

"Well, wasn't that somethin'?" Paddy asked Sarie.

She stared at him in muted awe. He had given up ... a *knighthood* ... to stay home with her and the baby! "Might I ... have the honor of a bit of a kiss, your lordship?" she asked him respectfully, and he obliged her. "Sir Padallor the Steadfast," said Sarie Clay proudly, and she kissed her husband again.

ſ

When Hollie arrived back at Castle Thraill, the first thing she asked for, after making the obligatory greetings to those who had gathered to welcome her, was to see her son.

Haldamar Tenet sent for Ronica to bring the baby, and she dutifully obeyed.

Clutching Owan tightly to her breast, Ronica crossed the floor to where Hollie stood, surrounded by those who greeted and those who had escorted her back from Blythecairne.

"Welcome home, dear," she said with forced enthusiasm. "We are so proud of you."

"Thank you, Ronica, for taking care of Owan for so long," Hollie replied.

"It was the sheerest pleasure for me," Ronica said honestly, and Haldamar added, "He was a joy to have around."

"May I take him?" Hollie asked, and Ronica nodded.

Owan looked suspiciously at the woman who reached for him, did not recognize her, and shrunk back against Ronica. He heard the woman say, "It's me, Owan—your mother," and turned away from her, burying his face in Ronica's bosom. He felt her hands lift him, and began to kick and cry.

The people in the little reception circle turned their faces away in embarrassment for Hollie, as Owan continued to cry and reach for Ronica. After Hollie held him for one frustrating, unfulfilling moment, Ronica said, "Perhaps ... after he gets to know you again...." Hollie handed him back to her sister-in-law, and the baby nestled against her, looking back at Hollie with anger and annoyance.

"Thank you," Hollie said, her heart pierced again.

Chapter Forty-One

It was late summer, and the kingdom of Hagenspan was enjoying its renewed peace. Families were gradually moving back to Solemon, grim but hopeful, replanting, rebuilding. A monument was planned for Solemon's town square to honor the brave, the foolish, the dead: a huge stone sword with its blade pointed toward the sky.

Hollie and Owan lived at Castle Thraill, in the same rooms they had dwelt in during the days when Roarke was alive. Owan had quickly warmed to the blue-eyed woman with the blonde shoulder-length hair, and was soon calling her "Mama." Aunt Ronica was a frequent visitor, as was Uncle Haldamar, who noticed his beautiful sister-in-law's pain and loneliness, and wished there were some way he could help.

Jesi Tenet and Alan Poppleton courted for awhile, sparred for awhile, courted a bit more, and finally parted in exasperation. Alan decided that Jesi was simply too young. He looked hopefully at Piper, but Piper Tenet had eyes for no man, choosing instead to spend her days in solitude, either in her room, reading or writing, or riding Buttercup through the hills, where she prayed and cried.

Esselte Smead eschewed the title of Lord, preferring to retain his title as the Steward of Thraill. He was a humble and generous leader, and even when word came reporting King Ruric's judgment that Marta Dressler had no part in Roarke's inheritance, Smead did everything he could to provide for her family—to provide not only for their material wellbeing, but also to create for her grandson Wylie a chance for greatness, as Marta had begged him.

༄

The sun cast long shadows over the garden, where Owan and Hollie played next to the stone dragon, surrounded by the fragrance of Ronica's flowers. Alan Poppleton appeared at the entrance to the garden, calling politely, "Lady Hollie! May I enter?"

"Of course, Alan."

"Master Smead sent me to find you. You have a visitor, back at the castle."

Hollie was intrigued. She had not known anyone was coming, and couldn't think who it might be. "Does this visitor have a name?"

"I expect so," Alan said with a grin, "but I came in after he had been announced, and I didn't get that information. A fast-talking fellow, small and wiry. He talks like he's not from around here."

Hollie gathered up her son and accompanied Alan back to the castle, curious and uneasy.

༄

"Hollie!" cried Kenndt, thrusting his arms into the air and running toward her. He wrapped her in an enthusiastic embrace, which she had no choice but to return, red-faced and repulsed, as Smead, the Tenets, two unfamiliar guards, and a few others stood nearby, watching.

Hollie smiled with restrained courtesy. "Why have you come here, Kenndt?"

"Heard about your misfortune," he said with a wink. "Come to comfort you."

"Misfortune...." Hollie repeated.

"Yes, the dragon, and old Roarke dying, and all that." Ronica Tenet shot him a livid, withering glower, and Owan toddled over to hug her around her knees.

"Ronica, could you watch Owan for a bit, while I talk to ... to Master Kenndt?" Hollie stammered, mortified.

"That'd be great," Kenndt accepted greasily. "Got a proposition for you."

"Come this way," she said hurriedly, pulling him from the hall and leading him toward the garden. Smead and Haldamar Tenet exchanged uneasy glances as they watched her leave.

ʃ

"I'm a rich man, Hollie, a rich man," Kenndt said in a cajoling tone. "I was rich before your Roarke paid for your freedom. He made me richer still. And now I'm even richer than that."

"I'm happy to hear you have been successful," Hollie said in a tone that suggested that she was not as happy as she professed.

"And you have been, too!" Kenndt said enthusiastically. "They say the king's awarded you Beale's Keep. That makes you a Lady, even if being old Roarke's widow didn't."

"I wish you hadn't come," Hollie said with a shudder.

223

"You won't feel that way after I tell you my plan." Kenndt smiled and took Hollie's hand before she realized what he was doing. "Marry me, Hollie!"

"What?" she said incredulously, and despite her aversion to her old employer, she laughed merrily. "I'm sorry, Kenndt—you can't possibly be serious!"

Undeterred, he continued, "With my gold, Hollie, and with your title … with your pretty face, and with my quick wits … what a pair we'd be!" He pulled her hand to his lips and kissed it. "We could take your little castle, and fix it up, and make it into the finest gambling house in the whole country. You could even run your own stable of girls, if that kind of thing would please you. Think of it!" he cried greedily. "I'd be a Lord!"

Hollie pulled her hand from his, looked firmly into his eyes, and declared, "Kenndt, hear me now: No. No. No. No. No." She frowned at him sadly. "No."

She turned to leave the garden. Kenndt, a little surprised at how quickly she had dismissed his proposition, said, "You'll change your mind, perhaps?"

She did not turn to look at him, just shook her head and kept on walking. "Goodbye, Kenndt."

"Will I see you at dinner tonight?" he called after her.

At that, she stopped, turned, and said to him, "You may stay here and eat tonight. Tomorrow morning you must leave."

"Not very damned accommodating," Kenndt muttered in frustration.

"I'll see you at dinner," Hollie replied.

"Well, Master Kenndt," Ronica Tenet said over a glass of red wine, "I understand it was at your Public House that my brother met our Lady Hollie."

"Yes, that's right. Very popular with the clientele."

"And she was waiting tables? What a humble position for one so beautiful!"

"That wasn't the humblest position she found herself in, if you know what I mean," Kenndt intimated, winking his eye at Roarke's sister. The other dinner guests who perceived what he was suggesting gasped, and the few women who didn't understand looked at their husbands and whispered, "What?"

Kenndt continued with a smirk, "Serving the tables wasn't the only job she did for me—no! Very popular with the clientele."

All of the blood drained from Hollie's face, and she fought to maintain control. "Piper," she asked, "will you please take Owan to my room?"

"Yes, Aunt Hollie," Piper said ruefully. "I'm sorry," she whispered, and Hollie smiled at her briefly, gratefully. At least her lips smiled … the look in her eyes was one of tormented pain.

Esselte Smead said grimly, "Captain Boole, would you please escort Master Kenndt from the grounds, and be sure that he doesn't accidentally injure himself on the way out?"

"With pleasure."

"Wait a bit! Wait!" protested Kenndt. "You don't understand. I actually proposed marriage to the whore, just this afternoon! I was willing to take her in, and give her a place of honor. And *this* is how I'm to be repaid?"

"With your permission, Master Smead?" Hess Boole asked.

Smead nodded, and Boole drew his sword.

"Wait! I'll leave! I'll go peacefully!" Kenndt spat, and he turned his chair over backward on the floor in his haste to get up and get away. The two bodyguards who had accompanied him to Thraill did not reach for their weapons, but arose and departed calmly, holding their hands aloft in the air where they could be easily seen.

"Lady Hollie," Smead apologized softly after they were gone, "Please … don't feel any shame. Don't feel any embarrassment from this unfortunate situation. You have nothing to explain to any of us." He smiled at her with great tenderness. "You are, and shall be, our Lady."

Hollie nodded sadly. "I should go check on Owan."

Ronica Tenet looked at her disdainfully through the narrowed slits of her eyes, then lifted her glass and sipped.

Chapter Forty-Two

"You haven't been around to see me very much lately," Hollie said to Piper, who stood at her doorway looking in.

"No. I'm sorry," she said awkwardly.

"Come in," Hollie urged.

"I shouldn't," Piper said. "Maybe just for a minute."

"Piper, what's wrong?"

The auburn-haired girl sighed. "It's Mother ... she told Jesi and me that we're not to spend time with you any more, without either Daddy or her being present."

Hollie's gaze drifted out the window. There were white, fleecy clouds wafting across a cerulean sky, white with just a hint of gray on their undersides. She wished she were among them.... How light she would be, how graceful, buoyed high toward the heavens, near the dwelling places of Cedric and God.

"I see," she said softly.

⌐

Esselte Smead knocked at the door to Hollie's room. She saw him standing there, and beckoned for him to enter.

"Hello, Owan," Smead said. "You're getting so big!"

Owan ran unsteadily across the room and hugged the legs of his friend Master Smead, who reached down and ruffled his corn-silk hair.

"How are you, Esselte?" Hollie asked.

"I've been a little worried about you, my dear."

"Yes … it's been hard."

"Ever since that man Kenndt came and attempted to dishonor you, I've been vexed for you," Smead said. "I wanted to protect you from the indignity you suffered."

"Thank you."

"Lady Hollie," Smead began, and stopped.

"Yes?"

"Forgive me. I have something to ask you, and I don't know how to do it. But I am the Lord of Thraill, officially … your son is my heir to this estate. And you yourself were formerly the Lady of Thraill, and would be so still, if only Cedric had had the time to amend his will. Or so I believe."

She waited for him to continue. He clasped his hands behind his back and went on.

"I told you once that you would always be the Lady of Thraill, in my estimation, or something like that. I'm not sure you completely understood what I was saying." His cheeks blazed red, and a bead of perspiration appeared on his forehead. "You don't need to answer me now—not if you need to think about it."

She realized what he was saying, and fought for the best way to formulate her answer.

Smead continued, "What I am saying is ... if it would please your heart to be the Lady of Thraill once again.... It might add a certain ... continuity, if you will, to the passing on of the estate. And I would be honored to share the Lordship with you." He glanced at her nervously. "I am babbling like a fool. You would not be forced to ... consummate the marriage, if you didn't choose to. It would be enough just to sit with you at table, to listen to you singing to the baby, to watch you brushing your hair." He patted his chest lightly. "Forgive me. Oh, my. I am a fool."

She reached out and took his hand.

"Whatever else you are, Esselte, you are no fool. I am very flattered that you would make an offer like this to one such as me." Smead started to protest, but she said, "Let me finish.

"Esselte, my friend ... I do not believe that I shall ever marry again. Maybe someday, I suppose, but right now, I can't see that far into the future.

"Cedric has been gone for just a year, and even though a year sounds like a long time ... that wound is still fresh to me. So ... thank you very much, with more sincerity than you can imagine, but ... no, my dear friend. I cannot."

Smead looked disappointed and relieved at the same time. "That's all right, my dear. I had to ask, you know." He smiled humbly. "What if I had not dared to ask, but you would have said yes? This is much better—much better."

Hollie reached up and kissed his face. "Thank you for understanding."

"You're quite a lady, my dear."

"And you, Master Smead—" she curtseyed and kissed the back of his hand, "you shall always be the Lord of Thraill to me."

"Thank you ... Hollie."

ʃ

It was winter, and Hollie was strolling through the garden while Owan played in the snow nearby.

Captain Hess Boole walked toward her, smiling and erect. "Lady Hollie!"

"Hello, Captain Boole." She liked this big, jovial man with his perpetually laughing eyes.

"Lady Hollie, I have a question for you."

"Well, ask it, then, and I shall do my best to have an answer for you," she rejoined.

"Yes, my Lady, I will. Here it is: I've a mind to try and court you, if there's the faintest chance in hell that you would ever agree to being seen in public with a galoot like me." He grinned at her, utterly confident in himself. "What do you think?"

Hollie's immediate reaction was a quick *no*, but then she realized suddenly that perhaps, just perhaps, she would enjoy sitting with Hess Boole and listening to his booming laughter as he told his tall tales and tweaked his companions. Of course, she could already do that, just about every night in the dining hall, but he was certainly suggesting something more ... intimate. And she considered the possibility that she might enjoy that, too.

But then she remembered her friend Esselte Smead, and knew that such a relationship would dishonor him, wound his pride, if not break his heart outright. And then she remembered her husband Cedric, and though she figured he would tell her it was all right ... she could not.

"No," she said quietly, her eyes downcast. "I don't think I could do that."

"That's all right, my Lady. That's all right. I just wanted to put the idea in your head and start it brewing." He smiled at her sincerely. "You didn't say 'forever', did you?"

"No," she realized, smiling faintly, "I didn't say that."

"Then, my Lady," he said, snapping off a crisp salute, "until tomorrow!"

ʃ

Hollie heard a knock at her doorsill.

"Who is it?" she called from her bedroom.

"It's Haldamar."

"I'll be right there," she said, wrapping a robe around her nightgown. "Is everything all right?"

"Oh, yes ... yes," Haldamar Tenet said in a nervous, distracted voice.

"Come in, and sit," Hollie said, concerned. "What is it?"

"It's spring," he said uncomfortably. He tried to smile then, to show her how relaxed he was.

"Yes, I know," she replied, smiling but a little apprehensive.

231

"Cedric has been gone now for a year and a half."

She nodded, looking at her brother-in-law, wondering what he was saying, and hoping she did not know.

"I just wanted to say, ah ... well," Haldamar cleared his throat, "you're a handsome woman, Hollie. A beautiful woman."

So softly he almost could not hear it, she said, "Thank you."

"And I just wanted to tell you ... well," Haldamar laughed, an unnaturally high giggle. "I guess I might just as well come out and say it."

She shook her head no, but it was so slightly that he went ahead anyway.

"If you ever ... feel the need for the, ah, for the company of a man ... I'd be honored if you'd think of me." He peeked at her to see if she seemed receptive. "No one would ever have to know."

"Oh, Haldamar," Hollie shook her head sadly. The burden of her beauty, of her femininity, felt like a leaden weight in her chest.

⚑

As Hollie lay in her bed that night, staring fretfully into the darkness, she suddenly knew what to do. She knew what it was that she *must* do.

It was spring. It was time for a new beginning.

It was time to take Owan and start living the rest of her life.

It was time to move to Beale's Keep.

Chapter Forty-Three

In the year since the Lady Hollie had left Castle Thraill, there had been just small changes at the fallen-down stone fortress of Beale's Keep, only minor improvements. No crops grew there that first summer, and little game came close enough to the castle to be able to hunt or trap.

But Esselte Smead sent monthly gifts from Thraill to supply Hollie and the small company that had gone with her. And when Blythecairne received word of Hollie's relocation to the center of neighboring County Temter, they also sent periodic gifts to help her get through that first winter.

Several soldiers from Thraill had accompanied Hollie to Beale's Keep, but they were not particularly adept at building. They were led by good-humored Hess Boole, who was appointed the Captain of the Guard of Beale's Keep. Boole and Hollie did not speak of romance, though sometimes their eyes would meet in an unguarded moment, and they would share a private, secret smile.

Yeskie, the woodsman from County Bretay who had led Yeskie's Brigade at Castle Blythecairne, now white-haired and halting of step, led a company of craftsmen from Blythecairne, and soon had a program under way for rebuilding Beale's Keep. Some people from Solemon, grateful for the sacrifices Hollie had made, arrived to settle in her district and help with the work. Alan Poppleton and his friend Brette also came to toil and build, after first having obtained permission from their fathers. Piper and Jesi Tenet would both have gone as well, but were not allowed.

ſ

"Mama?" Owan asked in a sleepy voice as Hollie was tucking his covers around him. The room was lit by the flickering light of a single candle in a brass holder.

"Mm-hmm," she hummed.

"Tully and Windy said I don't have a daddy."

"They did?"

"Yeah," he said, as he rubbed a fist into a droopy eye and tried to stifle a yawn.

Hollie bent over her son, ignoring his question, and kissed him on top of his silky golden head.

"So?" the little boy insisted.

"So what?"

"So, do I? Have a daddy?" He looked at her intently, his gray eyes trying to blink away the encroaching slumber.

"Of course, sweetie."

"Is it Cap'n Boo?" he asked eagerly.

"No," she smiled.

"Is it Uncle Alan?" he asked again, with only slightly less enthusiasm.

"No," she repeated.

"Well … who?"

"Your father," Hollie said softly, "was the noblest, bravest, most honorable man in the whole country. Maybe the whole world."

"Tell me."

"All right," she said, smoothing his blankets with the palms of her hands. "What do you want to know?"

"Did he ever do stuff?"

"Oh, yes!" Hollie laughed quietly. "Do you know what a dragon is?"

"Yeah. Uncle Alan told me."

"Well, a dragon was a very bad thing. Very, very bad. Much worse than Uncle Alan could ever have told you. Big, and mean, and scary. There used to be four dragons that lived here in our country." Owan smiled and quivered with vicarious fright.

"Your daddy was the bravest and the strongest and the best, out of all the brave and strong and good men who tried to kill those dragons. Your daddy was the only one who could."

The blond-haired boy was wide-eyed with awe. "My daddy beat all the dragons?"

"Well, three of them."

"What about the other one?"

She sighed, and then smiled at her son. "He was going to beat that one, too, but Iesuchristi called down to him and said, 'Let's have somebody else take care of that one. You come on up here with Me.'"

"Is that true?" the little boy demanded.

"Yes, it is," Hollie softly maintained. "Your daddy killed three dragons when nobody else in the whole world could …but somebody else had to kill the last one."

"Where is he now?"

Hollie breathed in deeply and exhaled slowly. It was all right. "He lives in God's country now. He's friends with Iesuchristi Himself."

Owan stopped to think about that for a moment. "Is he a hero?"

"Yes," she nodded.

"That's good." His eyelids grew heavier. "I like him."

"So do I," Hollie whispered.

She waited a moment, thinking that Owan had drifted off, but then his eyelids fluttered again, and he said, "Can I go see him someday?"

"Yes."

"I wish he'd send me a message." Owan knew about messages, for Alan Poppleton had just received a letter from Jesi Tenet a week earlier.

"You know ... your father did write you a message, just before he left for God's country. I still have it somewhere."

"Will you read it to me?"

"Maybe tomorrow." She laid her hand upon his brow, brushed the wisps of golden hair from his forehead. "Go to sleep now."

"All right," Owan mumbled. "I love you, Mama."

She kissed him on his downy cheek, and breathed, "I love you." Then she stood up from the bed, and sighed deeply. She retrieved the candlestick from the bed stand, and carried its softly dancing light from the room.

The End

also by Robert W. Tompkins

The Hagenspan Chronicles

Book One:
Roarke's Wisdom: The Defense of Blythecairne
Book Two
Roarke's Wisdom: The Courtship of Hollie
Book Three
Roarke's Wisdom: Going Home
Book Five
Kenyan's Lamp
Book Six
Owan's Regret: Widows and Successions
Book Seven
Owan's Regret: The Dragon King
Book Eight
Owan's Regret: Into the Wilds
and coming soon:
Book Nine
Owan's Regret: Peace of a Kind

non-fiction:

Disease and Faith
The Last Trumpet